# MECHS vs
# MUTANTS

Adapted by Steve Korté
Based on the screenplay *Mechs vs Mutants* written by
Kevin Burke & Chris Wyatt
Batman created by Bob Kane with Bill Finger

SIMON SPOTLIGHT
New York   London   Toronto   Sydney   New Delhi

SIMON SPOTLIGHT
An imprint of Simon & Schuster Children's Publishing Division
1230 Avenue of the Americas, New York, New York 10020
This Simon Spotlight paperback edition May 2017
All rights reserved, including the right of reproduction in whole or in part in any form.
SIMON SPOTLIGHT and colophon are registered trademarks of Simon & Schuster, Inc.
For information about special discounts for bulk purchases, please contact Simon & Schuster
Special Sales at 1-866-506-1949 or business@simonandschuster.com.
Designed by Nicholas Sciacca
The text of this book was set in Core Sans.
Manufactured in the United States of America 0417 OFF
10  9  8  7  6  5  4  3  2  1
ISBN 978-1-4814-9223-2 (hc)
ISBN 978-1-4814-9222-5 (pbk)
ISBN 978-1-4814-9224-9 (eBook)

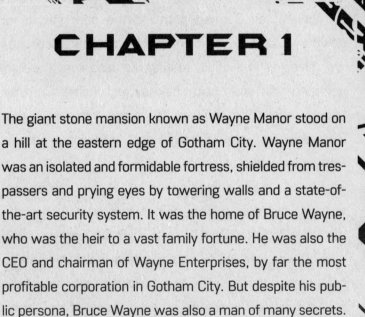

# CHAPTER 1

The giant stone mansion known as Wayne Manor stood on a hill at the eastern edge of Gotham City. Wayne Manor was an isolated and formidable fortress, shielded from trespassers and prying eyes by towering walls and a state-of-the-art security system. It was the home of Bruce Wayne, who was the heir to a vast family fortune. He was also the CEO and chairman of Wayne Enterprises, by far the most profitable corporation in Gotham City. But despite his public persona, Bruce Wayne was also a man of many secrets.

One of Bruce Wayne's secrets was that every night he became Batman, the crime-fighting Dark Knight of

Gotham City. Clad in a cape, a cowl, and a dark uniform, he prowled the city's dangerous streets and struck terror into the hearts of cowardly criminals and evil super-villains.

Another of Bruce Wayne's secrets was the location of Batman's secret headquarters. It could be found far below Wayne Manor, in a vast series of caverns known as the Batcave. Only Batman's closest allies were allowed to visit the Batcave, which was filled with high-tech equipment and vehicles that helped him keep the city's crime at bay.

Tonight, as Batman patrolled the dark streets of downtown Gotham City, one of his youngest associates was sleeping in a chair, resting his head over the Bat-computer. An open holo-book lay just inches from his fingers. Above the book was a holographic screen that was projecting pages from the book, showing images of Gotham's deadliest villains.

The teenager slumbering in front of the Batcomputer was Damian Wayne, the most recent hero to don the mantle of Robin the Teen Wonder. As Robin, Damian's main mission was learning all he could from Batman—how to fight, how to make a plan, how to keep his city and all the people in it safe. But at the moment, the only crime Damian was fighting was in his dreams. The soft sound of his snoring echoed gently through the Batcave as he slept.

Another person was creeping up behind him, walking carefully down the long flight of stairs and balancing a tea tray in his arms. It was Alfred Pennyworth, the dignified British butler who was one of the Dark Knight's most loyal allies. Alfred had practically raised Bruce since he had been orphaned as a boy. The butler was always there to help—whether he was helping Batman research a deranged villain, or simply preparing a late-night snack of Darjeeling tea and turkey sandwiches.

Alfred paused to gaze at Batman's dozing sidekick. The butler shook his head sadly, and then he cleared his throat.

"A-hem!" Alfred said loudly.

Robin's head shot up, and he quickly turned around.

"Oh, Pennyworth," he said with a yawn. "I was pulling an all-nighter, but I guess I fell asleep."

"Master Damian, as we have discussed on previous occasions, a young man must have adequate rest," Alfred said firmly. "Those who wore the Robin mask before you all made it a point to—"

"Save the *lectures*, please," Robin interrupted. "Don't tell me you didn't hear about what happened last night."

"Last night?"

"Oh, you really *didn't* hear?" asked Robin. "Well, don't

worry. The rest of the world sure has. Some guy on the street filmed it on his handheld device."

Robin let out a deep sigh as he reached forward and touched the holographic screen that floated inches above the Batcomputer. The screen instantly displayed a video labeled *Bird on a Wire*. The video showed Damian in his Robin uniform, standing high atop a building in downtown Gotham City. Next to him stood the Joker, one of Batman's deadliest opponents.

On the video screen, Robin yelled, "I've got him, Batman!"

The Teen Wonder lunged for the Joker, who deftly stepped to one side. Robin plunged over the edge of the building, falling fast until—

*ZZZZZIP!*

Batman quickly fired a roped Batarang toward his young partner, which wrapped around Robin's ankle and stopped his rapid descent. Seconds later, Robin was dangling upside-down, his cape covering his face as he swayed in the breeze.

"Hee-hee! Hoo-hoo!" the Joker laughed, pointing at Robin. "Now *that's* funny!"

*BLAM!*

Batman's fist slammed into the Joker's stomach, knocking the villain over.

As Robin struggled to free himself from the rope, he noticed a young boy on the street below him. The boy was pointing a video camera directly at Robin, recording his every move.

"Hey, stop *filming*!" Robin cried out in dismay.

The video clip went dark. In the Batcave, Robin muttered quietly, "Let's just say it's a pretty popular clip online."

Alfred nodded sympathetically and said, "I do see why this has caused you a measure of distress, Master Damian. But the Clown Prince of Crime has long been Batman's greatest enemy. It is not surprising that you found yourself at a disadvantage in your first encounter with him."

*"Disadvantage?"* Robin blurted. "I accidentally leaped off a building! If Batman hadn't been there . . ."

Robin paused to shake his head and continued, "I don't think Batman is too happy with me. I wish Tim was here. It would be good to talk to someone who's been through the Robin training before."

Tim Drake was the third young man to have fought crime as Robin, and he was Damian's immediate predecessor. Now Tim was fighting crime on his own as the hero Red Robin.

"It is unfortunate that Master Tim's work with his team keeps him away so much," Alfred agreed. "But you should speak with Master Dick. After all, he was the very first Robin."

"Yeah, but Dick Grayson has a whole new identity as Nightwing now," said Robin. "He's got his hands full. And besides, he's not really giving off the 'come talk to me' vibes right now."

*VROOOOOM!*

Robin and Alfred both looked up to see the Batmobile come roaring into the Batcave. The vehicle screeched to a halt on top of a revolving platform.

Batman jumped out of the Batmobile and approached his friend and apprentice.

"Master Bruce, I've prepared tea," said Alfred.

"Thank you, Alfred," said Batman as he glanced over at Robin. The young man was peering closely at the holographic book projection again.

"Studying?" said Batman. "That's good."

"That's what I was *trying* to tell Pennyworth," replied Robin. "I'm familiarizing myself with your biggest villains."

Alfred frowned and said, "*Not* good if it keeps him up all night, if I may say. And where have you been, sir?"

"On patrol," said Batman cryptically as he studied a

video screen on the Batcomputer. "Some trouble in the Bowery. Handled."

Robin pointed to his holographic screen. A short and stout man wearing a long coat and an old-fashioned top hat appeared on the screen.

"Hey, who's this little guy?" Robin asked with a chuckle.

"Oswald Cobblepot," said Batman. "The Penguin. Criminal kingpin."

"How come I haven't seen him around yet?"

"I sent him away," replied Batman. "I don't think we'll be seeing him for *quite* a while."

# CHAPTER 2

Over nine thousand miles away from Gotham City, in the vast and snowy expanse of Antarctica, the sound of a scratchy voice could be heard echoing off the ice-covered walls of a large cave. It was one of Batman's nemeses, the Penguin.

Deep within the cave the Penguin angrily trudged through snow, followed closely by an inquisitive penguin.

"That cursed Batman. It's all *his* fault!" squawked the Penguin. "Did I deserve this? Being stranded down here for over a year?"

Pausing at the edge of a frigid pool inside the cave,

the Penguin lowered a fishing pole into the icy waters.

"I just tried to make Gotham City a more livable place for criminals . . . *er* . . . people like me, and the Batman always ruins *everything*," he complained to his penguin companion. "*I* should be ruling Gotham City, not stuck in Mr. Freeze's lab of half-working machines."

Just then, the Penguin felt a movement on his fishing line.

"What? I actually caught something?"

With a vicious grin, he yanked on the fishing pole and reeled in a tiny minnow.

"Bah! Barely a mouthful!" he said with disgust, raising it over his mouth.

His penguin companion looked longingly at the fish dangling at the end of the line. The Penguin grunted and handed the tiny fish over to the hungry bird.

"You take it, Buzz," the Penguin said. "You know, you're the only one here I can talk to. You *understand* me."

"Buzzzzzz, buzzzzz!" agreed his feathered friend as he gobbled down the tiny treat.

A deep voice suddenly boomed from behind them. "Is it here? Where did I put those things?" the voice asked with irritation.

It was Mr. Freeze, the cold-hearted villain who had

once been a brilliant scientist named Victor Fries. A laboratory accident had changed his body chemistry so that he could only survive in sub-zero temperatures. He became the criminal known as Mr. Freeze, and he was forced to wear a bulky, life-sustaining freeze suit to stay alive. Today though, inside the frozen Antarctic cave, he did not have to wear his full freeze suit.

The Penguin turned around to glare at Mr. Freeze. "Oh great. Mister Fun is back."

The Penguin waddled over to him and asked, "What's got your thermals in a bunch, Freeze?"

Mr. Freeze barely glanced at the Penguin as he searched through a pile of laboratory equipment on a workbench.

"Solitude. That's all I ask for," he grumbled. "And yet *wretched humanity* keeps intruding upon me!"

"Wretched humanity?!" the Penguin sputtered. "If this is your way of saying you don't want me as a roommate anymore . . . the feeling is mutual! Just drop me off in Gotham City. I won't take it personally."

"No, not you, Penguin," Mr. Freeze said wearily. "My territory has been invaded!"

Mr. Freeze punched a button on a computer terminal, and a holographic image of a giant ocean oil-drilling platform popped into view.

An evil grin filled the Penguin's face as he said, "A new oil-drilling platform here on the ice pack? Maybe *they* can get me back to civilization."

"For the thousandth time, you will be much happier once you have turned your back on humanity," thundered Mr. Freeze as he continued to search through piles of mechanical devices. "Living among them brings nothing but misery! Ah, here we go."

With a smile, he reached for a three-pronged metallic device.

"What's that?" the Penguin asked as he strained to view the item in Freeze's hands.

"This arctic device is one of my inventions," Mr. Freeze replied as he attached the device to a large robotic arm. "And the key to our solitude!"

"*Our* solitude?" the Penguin muttered. "Oh great."

Mr. Freeze reached into a glass jar and extracted what looked like a big, brown bug. He placed it on top of a glass tray, directly below the robotic arm.

"My device can transform a simple animal, like this isopod, into a *monster!*"

As the Penguin and Buzz exchanged doubtful glances, Mr. Freeze walked confidently over to a computer terminal. He touched a few buttons, and the robotic arm began to hum. Suddenly, a bright blue light shot out of the arctic device and bombarded the isopod. The creature struggled to escape, but it was trapped within the light.

*ZZZZZZAAAAAAP!*

The isopod began to increase in size. Within seconds the creature had doubled, then tripled in size. Soon, it was the size of a school bus. The device detached from the robotic arm and clamped onto the back of the giant creature.

The isopod let out a fearsome roar as it crashed to the floor. The Penguin and Buzz backed away in horror.

"Yes!" cried out Mr. Freeze. "We shall defend what is *ours*! Come, beast!"

Mr. Freeze beckoned to the growling creature to follow him. Together, they moved toward the cave's entrance.

The Penguin turned to his feathered friend and said, "Come on, Buzz. We might as well see the show."

Across the ice pack a crew of workers was putting together oil drills, unaware of Mr. Freeze's approach. They were behind schedule, and working hard to get the giant oil-drilling platform up and running.

"Drill coming in!" one worker called. "Be ready for the setup."

A group of workers walked by with a huge beam, and another set with the drills. They all stopped when they saw Mr. Freeze on the cliff overlooking their work site.

"Your occupation of my land must come to an end!" Mr. Freeze's voice rang out defiantly across the snow-covered ridges of the Antarctic. "You shall return from whence you came!"

He shook his fist at the workers. The men on the platform simply looked at him with astonishment.

"Don't feign ignorance, you gadflies!" Mr. Freeze shouted. "Come here, my monster. *Attack!*"

*SCREEEEEECH!*

The giant isopod lumbered across the icy field and threw itself against the oil rig.

The workers fell back in terror, running away from the creature. The monster climbed onto the platform. With a flick of its tail, it knocked over a metal tower. The tower crashed to the floor of the platform and sliced open a large oil container. A wall of flames erupted from the spilled oil.

"Now, fools," shouted Mr. Freeze, "you know the consequences of crossing Dr. Victor Fries!"

The Penguin turned to Buzz and whispered, "Well, Mr. Freeze *is* crazy, but he's always entertaining."

"How could you even hope to defend yourselves?"

Mr. Freeze shouted at the workers. "You are powerless!"

"Well, Victor. They *are* roughnecks," the Penguin said. "They are obviously here to drill. And they might have—"

*VROOOOOOOOM!*

Before the Penguin could finish his sentence, the men emerged from a structure on top of the platform. They were pushing a giant machine that was topped with a large laser drill. The sound of the drill echoed across the snowy fields.

"Well, one of *those*," observed the Penguin.

Mr. Freeze laughed with contempt and called out, "Bah! How dare you defy me?!"

With an angry roar, the giant isopod lunged at the drill.

"Ready . . . aim . . . *fire*!" commanded one of the workers.

*ZAAAAAAP!*

A bright green laser shot out of the front of the drill and slammed into the isopod. The ray shattered the three-pronged arctic device that was still attached to the back of the creature. Pieces of the device tumbled into the snow.

The isopod cried out in pain and staggered backward. As the workers watched with astonishment, the creature began to shrink. Soon, it was no bigger than a mouse.

The workers burst out in cheers and laughter.

Mr. Freeze glared at them and shouted, "Laugh while you can! My next monster will *eradicate* you!"

Filled with rage, Mr. Freeze turned and headed back to the cave.

The Penguin stared at the damaged oil rig as smoke began to rise from the platform. He stroked his chin thoughtfully. A plan was already forming in his mind.

"*Next* monster?" he pondered as he waddled after Mr. Freeze. "Victor, wait!"

"Leave me alone! I need to plan," said Mr. Freeze as he entered the cave.

"You want better monsters?" asked the Penguin. "I think I can help."

Mr. Freeze stopped at the edge of a frozen pool and turned to glare at the Penguin.

"How?" he asked. "You had better be serious, Oswald."

"I've never been *more* serious," the Penguin said. "However, to pull it off . . . we have to return to Gotham City."

"Is this one of your tricks?" Mr. Freeze demanded.

"I assure you, far from it."

Mr. Freeze pondered for a moment, staring at the

Penguin's hopeful face. Then Mr. Freeze reached into his pocket and removed a remote-control device. He pushed a button.

*SPLASH!*

A giant submarine rose from the cave's icy pool. As it bobbed in the frigid water, a smile filled the Penguin's face.

"What are you waiting for?" demanded Mr. Freeze as he climbed onto the submarine. "To Gotham City!"

"Yes, to Gotham City!" the Penguin quickly agreed. He joyfully clambered to the edge of the machine.

"Buzzzzzz, buzzzzz!" came a sad sound from behind him.

"Why so sad, Buzz?" asked the Penguin as he turned to look at his friend. "You didn't think I would leave you behind, did you?"

The Penguin leaned closer to Buzz and whispered conspiratorially, "Besides, I need you to keep an eye on this madman for me."

# CHAPTER 3

Two nights later Robin was once again seated in front of an open book, viewing more holograms of Gotham's villains. Batman was standing nearby at the Bat-computer, analyzing data on a video screen. Alfred quietly approached.

"I'm confident, sir, that tonight's obligation to Wayne Enterprises is present in your thoughts," said Alfred.

"I haven't forgotten," replied Batman.

Robin looked up with interest and said, "The new technology showcase at Wayne Tower? That's tonight?"

"In less than ten minutes," Alfred replied.

"Isn't that super important?" asked Robin. "We'll never make it in time!"

"Yes, we will. Get in," said Batman as he calmly walked toward the Batmobile.

"Woo-hoo!" yelled Robin, his studies forgotten as he ran to the vehicle.

Batman fired up the Batmobile and said, "Alfred, you're on logistical support."

"Of course, sir."

Soon the Batmobile was zooming down a dusty road outside the Batcave that led to Gotham City.

"When do I get to drive?" asked Robin with excitement.

"We'll see," replied Batman.

"Soon?"

"We'll see."

"I hope it's soon," Robin said with a hopeful smile

Batman turned to Robin and said, "Remember, this is going to be a Wayne Enterprises function, so we have to wear our costumes."

"Got it . . . wait, what?" Robin said. "We're *already* wearing our costumes."

"These are our work uniforms."

"Huh?" asked Robin with confusion.

Later that night Damian found himself jostling against hundreds of well-dressed Gotham City citizens, all standing inside the Wayne Enterprises reception area. He tugged at the tight collar of his dress shirt and fidgeted inside his stiff custom-tailored suit.

"Stupid costume," he said with annoyance.

A waiter walked by with a plate of hors d'oeuvres. Damian picked up a cracker piled high with an unidentifiable slimy substance. He eyed it dubiously and then reluctantly put it in his mouth.

"Ack! Gross!" he said as he spat the item into a napkin. "Who would *eat* this?"

The sound of a man's laughter nearby caused Damian to look up in surprise.

"That *can't* be what it sounds like," said Damian. He turned in the direction of the laughter.

Damian's mouth fell open in disbelief. There was Bruce Wayne speaking with a group of people. He had a wide smile on his face and was laughing heartily.

"Hilarious, Madame Senator," said Bruce. "I'll definitely have to avoid *that* vintage!"

Damian muttered, "Whoa! He's so . . . *friendly!*"

A voice behind Damian whispered, "Yeah, it freaked me out the first time I saw it too."

Damian spun around to see Oliver Queen leaning over him. The wealthy industrialist Oliver Queen was secretly Green Arrow, the archer hero from Star City who often fought crime alongside Batman.

"Oh! Hi, Mister Green Arrow!" said Damian.

"Watch it, Damian!" Oliver said, glancing around. "Here it's Mister Queen. Call me Ollie."

Damian sighed and said, "Sorry, Ollie. Add that to the pile of rookie mistakes I've been making."

"Go easy on yourself, kiddo. We were *all* new once," Oliver said reassuringly. He waved a finger toward Bruce Wayne and added, "Plus, you're training under *him*. That's like jumping into the deep end . . . of the *ocean*!"

"Batm . . . um, the *boss* doesn't seem very happy with me," Damian said sadly.

"Not talking much? Acting grumpy?" asked Oliver.

"Yeah."

"That's just the way he is," Oliver said. "You know, Green Lantern took him to a 'theme planet' once. The whole planet was one big amusement park. I asked him how it was. You know what he said?"

Queen's amiable expression disappeared, and he formed his face into a perfect impression of Batman's grim demeanor.

"'Enjoyable.' That's all he had to say," Queen said with exasperation.

"Because he doesn't care," Damian offered.

"Wrong! It's the opposite," argued Queen. "Underneath he cares more than *any* of us. He has the biggest heart of all. I guess that's why he tries to hide it so well."

A distinguished-looking man wearing a military uniform approached Bruce Wayne.

"Mister Wayne, I presume," he said.

"Yes. You must be General Sam Lane," said Bruce as he shook the man's hand.

"You've done your research," Lane replied. "I'm responsible for the military's technology budget, and if today's demonstration goes as well as it's supposed to, I'm going to make you an even richer man."

"In that case, I'm *very* pleased that you're here, General," said Bruce with a smile.

The lights suddenly dimmed as two spotlights illuminated a stage at the front of the room. A nervous-looking man stepped up to a podium. While a large video screen was lowered behind him, the man spoke into a microphone.

"Ladies and gentlemen, if I could have your attention, please," he said. "I'm Dr. Kirk Langstrom, the head of the Wayne Enterprises Research and Development department."

The video screen was filled with the image of a large machine that was topped with a rotating drill.

Langstrom continued, "Wayne Enterprises has long produced high-tech drilling sledges for mining in extreme conditions. *Now* . . . welcome to the next level!"

The video screen lifted, and behind it stood a giant robot. Two powerful metal arms stood at the side of the machine, and at the end of each arm was a large gripping device. A massive block of stone was raised in front of the robot from beneath the stage.

"This is the single-operator Drilling Mech, and its plasma pincers actually turn solid rock into lava . . . allowing the mech to safely pass through," said Langstrom as he pointed to the machine. "Ready?"

A young man's face could be glimpsed within the robotic head plate, and the man nodded in response to Langstrom's question. The mech suit raised one arm in the air and pointed it at the large rock.

*ZZZZZAAAAP!*

A sharp blast of energy shot out of the mech's gripping device. Within seconds the gray rock was reduced to a fiery mass of red-hot lava. The mech then reached its hand inside the lava, plucking out a massive gemstone. The crowd gasped with astonishment.

"We designed this mech for mining exploration and extraction," Langstrom said. "But why limit it? Construction and military applications are just as possible."

*BEEP!*

Bruce Wayne reached for the mini-communicator in his pocket. Holding it to his ear, he whispered, "Alfred?"

"Emergency, sir," responded Alfred. "There has been a break-in at Arkham Asylum."

"You mean a break*out*?" asked Bruce. He scanned the room for Damian and found him a few feet back, also listening to Alfred's message.

"No, sir. *In*."

At the front of the room, Langstrom concluded his speech.

"This technology could one day be used to explore the core of the Earth or even other planets. The potential is nearly limitless. Thank you for your time."

General Lane applauded and turned to his companion to say, "Well, Mister Wayne, I have to say that I'm very impressed. You can—"

Lane looked around. There was no sign of Bruce Wayne.

"Anyone see where Mister Wayne went?" Lane asked with confusion.

# CHAPTER 4

Arkham Asylum was located on the outskirts of Gotham City. It was a dark and foreboding institution that sat high atop a desolate hill. Originally built as a mental hospital, Arkham had deteriorated over the years and become a poorly run prison. It was home to some of the most dangerous criminals in the world.

*RRRRRRINNNNG!*

Tonight the piercing sound of a security alarm filled the air as uniformed Arkham guards ran down a hallway, heading toward the maximum-security section of the asylum.

"Seal off the perimeter!" yelled a guard. "Full lock-down protocols! Get to your stations, people!"

The guard pushed a button, causing two heavy triple-layered metal doors to slam shut at the end of a corridor.

Another guard consulted a holo-screen and watched with alarm as it indicated the presence of an intruder inside Arkham. A deep rumble could be heard below them.

Peering at the screen, the guard said, "That's coming from—"

*KER-BLAM!*

The stone floor beneath the guards exploded into fragments as a giant tank-shaped drilling machine burst through the floor. The walls began to crumble, causing the guards to run for safety.

The tank climbed over a pile of debris and came to a rest inside the room. Mr. Freeze and the Penguin emerged from the machine and surveyed the rubble around them. Mr. Freeze was now wearing his protective freeze suit.

"Something tells me you don't have a license to drive this thing," the Penguin observed.

"No one can issue me a license, for there is no government that holds authority over Dr. Victor Fries!" replied Mr. Freeze as he hoisted a large freeze ray.

One brave guard pointed his laser weapon at the villains and called out, "Freeze!"

Mr. Freeze smiled and said, "Exactly."

*WHOOOSH!*

Mr. Freeze squeezed the trigger on his freeze ray and instantly covered the guard in a thick layer of ice.

As more guards came running down the hall, Mr. Freeze easily stopped each one with an arctic blast.

"In the name of the Gotham Police Arkham division, I demand that you give yourselves up!" yelled one icebound guard who was covered up to his neck in thick ice.

The Penguin waddled over and poked the ice-covered guard with his umbrella.

"You're the best that Arkham has to offer?" the Penguin said with a sneer. "It's embarrassing that I've ever been kept in here."

"Stay focused, Cobblepot," said Freeze. "You promised me what we need is somewhere in here. I've already spent more time among other humans than I'm comfortable with."

"Oh, you won't be disappointed," replied the Penguin as the two villains made their way down Arkham's hallway.

They soon came to the first cell. Inside it was a desperate-looking inmate, his head covered with bandages. The prisoner put his hands against the glass window of his cell and pleaded, "Release me—I shouldn't be in here!"

"That's what they *all* say," the Penguin muttered, and walked away.

At the next cell they found a smiling man who was wearing a tall green top hat and a large bowtie. He was jumping up and down in excitement. It was the Mad Hatter.

"What are you guys doing trapped in that hallway?" he called out. "Don't you want to be free in here . . . like me?"

"Okay, freak show," replied the Penguin as they continued down the hall.

Cheetah leaped at her cell door as they passed by, still furious at the Penguin for abandoning her during the last criminal scheme they'd pulled together.

Inside the next cell the villain Two-Face had just flipped a coin in his hand, trying to decide what he should do. He stared at the coin and said, "I don't deserve to be free of here."

"I was going to say the same thing," said the Penguin, nodding his head in agreement.

"Where are the *items* we need?" Mr. Freeze asked angrily.

"Patience, Victor," said the Penguin. "I waited for months in your mad scientist igloo. You can wait a few moments more."

Minutes later they arrived at a thick metal door with no window.

"First on the list . . ." said the Penguin as he pointed his umbrella toward the door.

Mr. Freeze aimed his freeze ray directly at the door's computer locking system.

*WHOOOSH!*

A blast of ice disabled the lock, allowing the Penguin to slide the door open. They stepped into the cell and stood in front of the villain known as Bane. One of Batman's most dangerous foes, Bane's body was filled with the dangerous substance known as Venom, a poison that gave him superstrength. Tonight, his muscles gleamed in the dim light of his cell, but he was tightly restrained with metal clamps over his giant arms.

"What do you two want?" Bane demanded.

"Time to come with us, Bane," said the Penguin.

"Why do you want me out?"

*WHOOOSH!*

A blast of frozen energy shot out of Mr. Freeze's weapon, shattering the manacles around Bane's arms.

With a smile, Bane flexed his biceps and pounded his fists together.

"Explanations in good time," said the Penguin. He turned toward the next cell. "Or we can always close you back in."

Soon the three villains had expanded their ranks to five. Joining them were Chemo, a large green chemical-infused monster, and Killer Croc, a massive half-crocodile, half-human villain.

"One more to go," said the Penguin.

After the next cell door was blasted open, Mr. Freeze stepped inside and looked around.

"This cell is *vacant*, you fool," he said to the Penguin.

"Au contraire," replied the Penguin.

*SLLLLLURRRRRP!*

A thick brown sludge began to ooze out of one corner of the cell. The substance quickly rose and took the form of Clayface, the shape-shifting monster capable of assuming the form of almost anything or anyone.

"Clayface, meet your new boss, Mr. Freeze," said the Penguin.

As the six villains made their way down the dark hallway, a high-pitched voice called out to them.

"Now, you wouldn't forget little ol' *me* in your escape

plans, would you? Because that wouldn't be funny, if I do say so myself."

The Penguin was pulled to a stop when two purple-gloved hands burst through the bars of a cell and grabbed onto the collar of his coat. The Penguin turned to glare at the Joker, who flashed a wide grin.

"Sorry, clown. I already have to deal with one lunatic on this job," said the Penguin. He struggled to free himself.

"Ozzie, Ozzie, Ozzie. You need me," argued the Joker. "I'm the *style*. I'll put the life in your team's party."

The Penguin reached for his umbrella and quickly slammed it against the Joker's hands. As the Joker giggled uncontrollably, he fell back into his cell.

"I would get used to your accommodations, if I were you," taunted the Penguin as he walked away.

"I have an absolutely awful memory, Oswald. But *this* I won't forget! *Do you hear me?!*" shouted the Joker as the six villains moved down the hall.

Not far from them, two dark figures stood on a ledge above the entrance to Arkham Asylum. Batman's cape billowed in the wind as Robin looked on impatiently.

"Why are we waiting?" asked Robin.

"I'm scanning," said Batman, focusing the thermal cameras located inside his cowl to search inside the building. "Always use caution, Robin. Leaping into Arkham unprepared is like going into a lion's den."

*WHOMP!*

A cabled arrow shot past Batman and Robin and imbedded itself in the stone wall.

"I've always loved the lion's den," said Green Arrow as he swung through the air and crashed through a window. The hero tumbled to the floor inside and called out, "It's my favorite part of the zoo."

Robin turned to Batman and said, "I'm thinking he's not great at *caution*."

Batman's mouth tightened into a frown.

"Let's go," he said as he and Robin jumped through the window and entered the asylum.

*WHOOOSH!*

Down the hall Mr. Freeze blasted a heavy metal door with ice. The door tumbled to the ground, and the Penguin and the other villains stepped into view.

"What did I say? Checking off everything on our shopping list was easy," the Penguin said with a chuckle.

Bane turned to glare at Killer Croc and said angrily, "Wait, you don't expect me to work with this *snake*, do you? He sold me out to the Gotham Police."

Killer Croc pushed his scaly face up to Bane's and replied, "You got a score to settle with me? Then let's settle it!"

"Gentlemen, now is not the time," the Penguin said, "We should be on our way before Batman—"

Before he could finish his sentence, a roped Batarang flew through the air and looped itself around the Penguin. With a quick tug, Batman pulled on the rope and yanked the Penguin off his feet.

"This game ends now," declared Batman.

"Game?" sneered Mr. Freeze. "Trust me, we are *not* playing."

Green Arrow dropped to the ground behind the villains and nocked an arrow to his bowstring. "Really? Because I could go for a round of pin the arrow on the bad guy. Who wants to go first?"

Robin felt a hand on his shoulder. Startled, he turned to see Commissioner Gordon, the head of the Gotham City Police Department, standing next to him.

"Good work, Robin. We'll take it from here," said the commissioner.

"Gordon?" said Robin with surprise. "How did you make it to Arkham so quickly?"

"Kid, duck!" called out Green Arrow as he drew a special arrow from his quiver and pointed it directly at Gordon.

Robin jumped in front of the commissioner. "Are you crazy?" he yelled.

"Do it *now*!" commanded Batman.

As Robin watched with horror, the man he thought was Commissioner Gordon slowly began to morph into a puddle of brown mud. It was Clayface! The monster swung a giant fist at Robin; he barely managed to roll out of the way in time.

"This guy wasn't in my holo-book of villains!" protested Robin.

Green Arrow leaped to the side to avoid being hit by Bane's giant fist. As the hero loaded an arrow into his bow, he turned to Robin and asked, "You're learning how to be a super hero from a book?"

*ZIP!*

Green Arrow fired an arrow at Killer Croc, but it shattered against his scaly body.

Robin threw a punch at Clayface, but the teen's arm sank into the monster's squishy stomach. As Robin delivered a roundhouse kick to Clayface's . . . well, clay face, the monster easily knocked the hero aside.

"We're wasting time!" called out Mr. Freeze, raising his freeze ray.

*WHOOOSH! WHOOOSH! WHOOOSH!*

Mr. Freeze rapidly fired his weapon, creating an impenetrable wall of ice around the six villains.

"Great, you've trapped us in here!" complained the Penguin.

Mr. Freeze turned to glare at the Penguin and said, "You *are* a short-sighted little man."

*WHOOOSH!*

Mr. Freeze blasted the floor next to them, cracking it open with thick ice.

"Bane, *now*!" he commanded.

With a grunt, Bane lifted his massive arms in the air and then smashed them down against the icy floor. A giant hole opened below them. One by one, the six villains jumped through the gaping hole in the floor.

Green Arrow fired arrow after arrow into the towering wall of ice. After the ice finally cracked open, the heroes rushed in.

Batman frowned as he trained his thermal cameras into the floor below them.

"They escaped," he said. "There are sewer tunnels underneath here. They had a vehicle waiting. They're gone."

Robin shook his head with dismay and muttered, "This wouldn't have happened if I could tell the difference between the real Gordon and Clayface."

Green Arrow put a reassuring hand on Robin's shoulder. "You're still learning, kid."

"I guess," Robin said with a sigh.

# CHAPTER 5

Back at the Batcave, Batman was intently staring at screens on the Batcomputer. Images of the six villains filled the screens. Nearby, Robin was studying his holo-book of villains. Standing behind both heroes, Green Arrow lazily sharpened his arrows.

"What's the big mystery?" asked Green Arrow. The situation seemed pretty straightforward to him. "Penguin and Mr. Freeze needed some muscle and freed some inmates. Simple as that."

"On the surface, it looks simple," replied Batman.

"You think there's a pattern here?" asked Robin.

"The breakout wasn't random," said Batman. "They skipped other inmates to select Bane, Chemo, Croc, and Clayface. Why *them*? It's not a solid team. Bane and Croc have a known rivalry."

"We don't need to know what they want," argued Green Arrow. "We just need to stop them."

"The key to stopping them is outsmarting them," replied Batman.

"Unless you have explosive arrows," Green Arrow said with a smile as he fondled a handful of explosive arrows. "Then *that's* the key to stopping them. Oh, and look what *I've* got!"

Robin continued to study his book, looking at pictures of the six villains.

"A pattern . . . ?" he pondered.

Deep beneath the Gotham Harbor, hundreds of feet below the water's surface, a long-forgotten cavern sat at the end of one of the city's sewer lines. The Penguin and his criminal companions had made this secret lair their headquarters. Tonight Mr. Freeze was laboring over a massive machine in the middle of the cavern. Bane, Chemo, and Clayface were all reclining on lab tables, their arms and legs encased in heavy metal clamps to prevent movement.

Thick rubber tubes extended from their arm clamps, connecting each villain to the giant machine.

Bane glared at Mr. Freeze and grumbled, "If this is a trick—"

Before he could finish, Mr. Freeze sighed and said, "You will no doubt inflict bodily injury upon me. Yes, yes. Your threats are *de rigueur*. Do not worry. My science is no hoax."

The Penguin absentmindedly reached down to pat Buzz on the head, which drew the interest of Killer Croc.

"What's that little guy's name?" asked Croc. "Is it *Appetizer*?"

"Buzz is my hench-bird," the Penguin snapped, and then turned to his feathered friend to say, "Don't mind him, Buzz. He's a mere sewer-born cretin."

Killer Croc leaned closer to the Penguin and said, "Level with me, Penguin. What are the odds this is going to work?"

"Victor Fries is a loony with a monster-size ego," the Penguin said. "He's practically a hermit, and on top of it all, he's a terrible roommate. But he's also one other thing."

"What's that?"

"A genius," said the Penguin.

Mr. Freeze turned to a control panel and opened a large holographic screen. He then placed his open palm on top of the screen.

"Time for the moment of truth," he said.

*BOOOOOM!*

The cavern was filled with a deafening roar as machines activated and chemicals began to flow through the tubes. The chemicals traveled from the arms of the three villains and flowed through the tubes and into the machine. Each tube contained a deadly poison: Bane's Venom, Chemo's chemicals, and Clayface's mud. The villains screamed in agony and writhed in pain on the tables.

Above them all, the central core of the machine blinked alive.

In the Batcave, Batman was growing more and more frustrated as he stood in front of the Batcomputer and studied the profiles of the six villains.

"Criminal history: no connection," he read. "Known M.O.'s: no connection. Personality profile: no connection."

"Maybe they're just recruiting for an all-villain flag football league?" offered Green Arrow as he sipped a cup of tea.

Robin looked up from his book and asked, "What if Penguin and Freeze didn't pick these guys for who they are . . . but instead, for what they're *made* of?"

"Made of?" said Green Arrow. "What does it matter?"

"Never mind," said Robin as he turned back to his book. "Probably nothing."

"Tell me," said Batman.

"Well," Robin began hesitantly, "three of them have unusual chemical components. Bane has Venom, the stuff that makes him strong."

Robin continued, "There's Clayface's mud, which can expand into anything. And Chemo? Well, he's basically made of supertoxic sludge."

"What about Croc? He's not like the others," said Green Arrow.

"No, but the strength of his constitution would make him an ideal test subject," Robin said. "Mr. Freeze is a scientist, right? What if he's experimenting with—"

"No offense, kid," Green Arrow interrupted. "But don't you think that's a bit of a stretch?"

Batman shook his head firmly and said, "No."

"Okay, dumb idea," admitted Robin.

"I mean, no, it's *not* a stretch," replied Batman.

A smile spread on Robin's face as he said, "It's not?"

Batman turned around to face Robin.

"I was focusing on the villains' *skills*," said Batman. "It never occurred to me to analyze their physical composition. Good work, Robin."

Batman started punching keys on the Batcomputer, calling up diagnostic scans of the six villains.

"To force those kinds of chemicals to interact with one another, there would be tell-tale signs in chroma-spectral scans of the area," he said.

The Batcomputer emitted a chiming sound.

"Got a hit," said Batman.

The Dark Knight immediately started moving toward the Batmobile.

"Robin, with me," he commanded.

"Where to?" asked Robin.

"Gotham Harbor," said Batman as he hopped into the Batmobile.

"I'll follow in a second," called out Green Arrow. "In the meantime, this cup of tea is getting low."

He waved his cup in the air, hoping to attract Alfred's attention.

Alfred frowned as he poured more tea into the cup and said, "Indeed, sir."

The echoes of the roaring machine and the screams of the three villains strapped to the tables caused the Penguin to cover his ears. The flow of chemicals traveling from the villains to the machine continued to accelerate.

All three liquids mixed together within the machine's central chamber. Finally, Mr. Freeze punched a button on the machine's control panel.

"It is done," he said.

He walked over to the machine, opened a panel, and removed a thin glass tube. Inside the tube was a thick, bubbling purple stew of chemicals from the three villains.

"How will you know if it worked?" asked the Penguin.

"There's only one way to find out," said Mr. Freeze as he loaded the tube into an injector.

Killer Croc smiled and said, "Lay it on me."

With a grim smile, Mr. Freeze pushed the injector up against Croc's scaly bicep.

*WHOMP!*

The purple chemicals flowed from the injector into Croc's arm.

Croc closed his eyes and swayed on his feet.

"Yes! I feel it!" he growled. "The *power*!"

Killer Croc began to shake. Then he began to expand. Soon, he doubled in size. Then he doubled again. And again.

The other villains watched in amazement as Croc towered over them, growing to fifty feet in height!

*ROOOOOOAAAAAR!*

The cavern shook as the giant Killer Croc spread his massive arms and stomped his giant feet on the ground.

"It's time to have a little fun!" he roared.

# CHAPTER 6

The waters of Gotham Harbor were calm tonight. A full moon illuminated a small boat floating offshore. A bearded sailor hummed quietly as he slowly dipped his fishing rod into the water.

Suddenly, the waters below the boat began to churn. The man looked up in surprise to see a large wave forming in the distance. The boat began to rock, knocking the sailor off his feet. Another giant wave erupted in the water and flooded over the prow. The sailor crawled to the edge of the boat and peered into the swirling water. Something below the boat was moving closer to the surface!

*SPLAAAAAASH!*

The boat rocked violently in the harbor, and the sailor fell back in horror. Killer Croc emerged from the water's murky depths, water dripping off his scaly skin. He now stood over one hundred feet tall and was still growing. He opened his mouth to display razor-sharp fangs—each the size of a full-grown man!

With a harsh laugh, Croc bellowed, "It's time to have a little fun." It was also time to see if Mr. Freeze's serum worked. Killer Croc then dipped his giant head into the harbor and began to swallow massive amounts of water.

His mouth dripping with water, Croc stalked to the shore. He opened his mouth to spit out a steady stream.

*WHOOOOOOSH!*

An arctic blast of ice and slushy snow shot out of the monster, flying high over the buildings of Gotham City. Snowflakes floated down to the streets, and the shoreline was quickly covered in ice.

Croc smiled at the wintry scene before him, and then he dipped his head back into the water to gather another mouthful.

*WHOOOOOOSH!*

A dusting of snow lightly covered downtown Gotham City. Confused pedestrians, still wearing their summer outfits of shorts and T-shirts, shivered as the snow fell around them. Delighted children threw snowballs.

*WHOOOOOOOSH!*

A massive blast of icy snow slammed into a group of pedestrians, knocking them over. A family of tourists ran inside a nearby office building seconds before an avalanche of snow came crashing down.

Minutes later nearly all of the buildings in downtown Gotham City were covered in ice and snow. Snowdrifts piled up in front of doors, trapping some of Gotham City's citizens inside the buildings. Others slipped and fell outside on the slippery streets.

*VROOOOM!*

Suddenly, the loud roar of the Batmobile could be heard as it zoomed through downtown Gotham City.

Inside the vehicle Batman looked grim as he navigated the icy streets. Robin pressed his face up against the window, his mouth open wide in astonishment.

"Hey, do super heroes get snow days?" asked Robin.

Batman's mouth tightened into a frown.

"That's a no, I guess," said Robin.

Robin continued to survey the snowy scene and said, "Sudden weather shift. Icy conditions. Part of Mr. Freeze's plans, I assume?"

"No doubt," replied Batman.

"You know, if you let *me* drive," Robin offered, "you could focus on developing the perfect plan for fighting Freeze."

"Not the time, Robin."

Robin sighed and looked out the window again. Off in the distance, something caught his attention.

*THUD! THUD! THUD!*

It was the giant Killer Croc, now nearly as tall as Gotham City's highest skyscrapers. Buildings shook as the monster marched through the city.

"Uh, you're seeing this, right?" asked Robin.

"Like you said, Chemo's acid mutates," Batman said grimly. "Clayface's mud stretches. Bane's Venom enlarges."

"But I didn't know that meant *giant crazy monster*!" protested Robin. "*Now* what do we do?"

*EEEEK!*

People were screaming in horror as Killer Croc stomped through the snow, almost crushing one family. The monster grabbed on to the top of a nearby building and easily yanked it off its foundation.

"Now, let's cause some chaos!" he said with a laugh as the building shattered into pieces and tumbled to the ground.

Just then, Croc spied the Batmobile charging directly at him.

"What's this? An old friend?" Croc roared with delight. "I should spend some time with him, now that I've come *up* in the world!"

The Batmobile was moving closer and closer to the giant monster. Robin's eyes widened with fear.

"You wearing your seat belt?" asked Batman.

"Always," Robin replied nervously.

"Good."

Batman shifted into high gear, and the Batmobile sped ahead. It was on a direct collision course with Killer Croc.

The monster smiled and said, "Oh yeah? Bring it!"

*ZOOOOM!*

Suddenly, a bright red blur appeared next to the Batmobile. It was The Flash, the red-suited super hero who was the Fastest Man Alive. The Flash was one of Batman's closest allies.

"Hey, guys!" he called out to Batman and Robin as he ran alongside the Batmobile. "A minute ago I was having coffee in Paris when I saw the news. Sorry it took me so long to get here!"

*WHOOOOOOSH!*

Killer Croc opened his mouth wide and exhaled an icy

blast of snow in front of the Batmobile. Batman expertly navigated the skidding car and pushed a button on the vehicle's dashboard. Sharp spikes erupted from the car's tires and gripped the icy road.

The Flash was less lucky. Sliding down the street, he frantically waved his arms in the air in an effort to maintain his balance.

"Hey, what the—" he yelled out, tripping over a mound of snow and then crashed into a Dumpster.

"There goes The Flash," observed Robin.

*BLAM! BLAM! BLAM!*

Three black missiles shot out of the front of the Batmobile and exploded against Killer Croc's armorlike scales.

"What?! *Aughhh!*" the monster cried out in pain.

The Batmobile executed a quick turn on the icy street, but Killer Croc was too fast. He reached down and easily lifted the vehicle into the air like it was a toy. The monster's angry eyes narrowed as he peered into the vehicle.

"Um, hi, Mister Croc," said Robin nervously. "Good to, um, see you?"

Killer Croc smiled and said, "Good-bye for good, Batman!"

Croc hurled the Batmobile through the air, launching it toward a skyscraper.

"I can't watch this," Robin said with a moan as he covered his eyes.

Batman calmly pushed another button on the dashboard.

The wheels of the Batmobile retracted, and sleek black wings emerged from the sides of the vehicle.

*ZOOOOOM!*

The Batmobile had transformed into a sleek plane. Batman effortlessly piloted the flying vehicle up and over the buildings in downtown Gotham City.

Robin opened his eyes and yelled with delight, "It turns into a *plane*?! This is the coolest thing *ever*!"

Batman gave only the tiniest smile of satisfaction.

Robin looked out the window of the Batwing and observed that large portions of the city were now covered in snow and ice.

"Any chance this thing also transforms into an enormous heat lamp?" he asked.

"If we stop the monsters, the climate will go back to normal," said Batman.

"Right. Wait . . ." Robin said with confusion. "*Monsters?* As in more than one?"

"Look down," said Batman.

Robin's mouth fell open with shock. Standing at the

edge of the harbor was Chemo, now almost as large as Killer Croc. One of his arms was submerged in the water, and his other arm was pointed toward the city.

*WHOOOOOOSH!*

A frigid mixture of ice and slush shot out of Chemo's arm, covering more of the city in snow.

"Freeze is turning Gotham City into the Arctic," Batman said grimly.

Mr. Freeze was studying four holographic screens in the cavern below Gotham Harbor. Each one showed the ice and snow cascading over Gotham City.

"It's better than I could have ever hoped," he said with a smile. "Soon I won't need this blasted suit to cool me down anymore."

The Penguin walked up to him and said, "What did I tell you, Victor? You were so focused on defending your little ice cave, you weren't thinking *big*!"

"Yes, you're right," Mr. Freeze said. "I *have* been underestimating myself, haven't I?"

"Oh yes, Victor," agreed the Penguin. "Look at those screens. See *all* that you can accomplish."

Mr. Freeze was so engrossed watching the screens that he didn't notice the Penguin handing off a tiny glass vial to Buzz. The little bird quietly waddled over to the giant machine in the middle of the cavern and pressed his beak up against a panel in its side. He inserted the vial into the machine. As the Penguin watched nervously, the machine deposited the purple stew of chemicals that had been collected from Bane, Clayface, and Chemo inside. Buzz then tucked the vial under one of his flippers and hid it there.

The Penguin sighed with relief as Buzz waddled over to the other side of the laboratory, carrying the vial out of the room. An evil grin filled the Penguin's face as he followed Buzz.

# CHAPTER 7

Gotham City was now an arctic wasteland. Snow covered nearly every building and vehicle. Gotham City's citizens shivered in the freezing cold weather as they cautiously made their way down the icy sidewalks in an attempt to escape the chaos.

*RUMMMMMMBLE!*

A huge pile of snow atop an office building began to crumble. A young man and woman stumbled on an icy sidewalk, right below the building. They looked up in horror as the snow tumbled toward them.

*ZIIIIIP!*

Atop a nearby building Green Arrow drew back his bowstring and shot a cabled arrow toward them. The cable wrapped around the couple, and Green Arrow gave a sharp tug on the line. The man and woman were whisked up into the air and out of the way of the cascading snow.

"*Help!* Someone help me!"

Green Arrow looked down the street to see an avalanche of snow descending on a tiny, frightened old woman. She was running as fast as she could, but the snow was gaining on her. Green Arrow would not be able to reach her in time.

*WHISK!*

A red-and-black blur shot through the air, passing by Green Arrow. It was Nightwing, swinging on a rope from a nearby rooftop. As the hero flew closer to the ground, he effortlessly caught the woman in his arms and swung her to safety.

"Nightwing! Thank you!" the woman said. "Such a good boy."

"No, problem, ma'am," Nightwing said politely. A crowd of people gathered around them.

Green Arrow joined them and pointed to a nearby bank that had not been completely iced over.

"You all need to find safety indoors," he said.

As the crowd moved toward the bank, Nightwing spoke with Green Arrow.

"An avalanche in downtown Gotham City?" asked Nightwing.

"Give you one guess who's behind this," Green Arrow replied. "And it rhymes with *sister, please.*"

"How did Mr. Freeze get power on this scale?" wondered Nightwing.

"Ask Batman—or the new Robin—for details," said Green Arrow. "But I, for one, never wanted to live in a snow globe."

*THUD! THUD! THUD!*

The giant Killer Croc stomped down a nearby street, crushing cars and smashing into buildings. Nightwing's mouth hung open in astonishment.

"Oh yeah," said Green Arrow with a shrug. "And then there's that."

In the middle of downtown Gotham City an ominous rumble could be heard. It was Mr. Freeze's massive ice tank rolling down the frozen streets. Within the tank sat Mr. Freeze, the Penguin, Clayface, and Bane.

Mr. Freeze turned to the Penguin and said, "Thanks to you, I realize I don't have to hide from civilization. I can turn civilization into what I want! An ice world!"

The Penguin raised an eyebrow and said, "Ice world? Not everywhere, I hope. After all, I didn't buy my own private island just so it could freeze over."

"Of *course*, everywhere," said Mr. Freeze with annoyance. "Now, because of you, I think *big*. A new global *ice age*!"

As Mr. Freeze laughed maniacally, the Penguin shook his head with disgust.


At the edge of Gotham Harbor, the Batwing swooped through the air, circling the giant Chemo. The monster continued to spew ice and snow throughout the city.

*BLAM! BLAM! BLAM! BLAM!*

The Batwing fired four missiles at Chemo. They exploded on top of the monster but had no effect.

"He doesn't even seem to know we're here!" said Robin.

"Then it's time to drop the subtlety," said Batman.

"A barrage of missiles is *subtle*?"

Batman pulled back sharply on the Batwing's yoke, causing the craft to shoot straight up in the air. Batman then pushed a button on the control panel.

"What are you doing?" asked Robin. "Isn't that the button that turns off the jets?"

"Yes," replied Batman.

"Wait, why would you—" began Robin.

Before he could finish his sentence, the Batwing started falling. It picked up speed as it fell. Seconds before the craft was about to land on top of Chemo's head, Batman pushed the button again. The jets at the back of the Batwing roared into action. Searing hot flames shot out of the Batwing and singed Chemo's head. The monster roared in anger.

"There," said Batman. "He noticed us."

Chemo pointed his arm toward the Batwing and shot a storm of ice directly at the craft.

"I think you made him mad!" observed Robin. The Batwing was spiraling out of control. Within seconds it was plummeting toward the ground.

Batman pulled back on the yoke with all his strength. Just as the Batwing was about to crash into the icy street, the craft transformed back into the Batmobile. It zoomed down the icy street and then came to a stop.

"You know what?" Robin said wearily. "Maybe I *don't* want to drive this thing anymore."

THUD! THUD!

The monstrous Killer Croc was heading directly

toward the Gotham City Police Department headquarters. Commissioner Gordon and a dozen officers were standing on the roof of the building. The officers were armed with laser weapons. An array of tanks was lined up on the street.

"Officers, open fire!" called out Gordon.

*ZAAAAAP! BLAM!*

Lasers and tank blasts bombarded Killer Croc. The monster roared in anger, but he brushed off the assault. At his normal size Killer Croc's scaly skin acted as a thick, almost impenetrable armor. Now that he was huge, his scales had only become tougher; there was no way this barrage of blasts could hurt him.

"It's not affecting him!" Gordon called out.

Killer Croc opened his mouth and covered the tanks in a thick layer of ice.

Croc smiled as he broke off a chunk of the building's roof and threw it toward the officers.

"Smashing up the Gotham City Police Department!" Croc bellowed. "I *knew* this day would come!"

Croc moved toward the roof, one giant claw reaching out to grab the frightened police officers. Thinking quickly, Gordon ran over to the Bat-Signal, the large machine that projected the silhouetted shape of a bat in the sky to call for help from Batman. Gordon switched it on, and the machine's bright light pierced the nighttime sky. He then swiveled the machine so that the light shone directly into Killer Croc's face. The monster cried out in annoyance, unable to see. He blindly slammed his giant fists against the building.

Just then, The Flash appeared on the roof.

"Need a lift?" he asked as he quickly gathered the police officers in his arms and raced them to safety.

"At least my officers are safe," said Gordon with a sigh of relief. He looked up just in time to see Croc's massive hand come crashing down toward him.

*ZIP!*

Nightwing swung into action, hanging from a Batrope. He grabbed Gordon and flew him to safety.

"We would *never* forget you, Commissioner!" said Nightwing. He fired another grappling line and soared through the air.

Killer Croc roared with frustration.

# CHAPTER 8

Mr. Freeze stood outside his ice tank in the middle of Gotham City, grimly observing the icy landscape. Buzz cavorted on top of a nearby snow bank, burrowing happily beneath the surface. The Penguin, Clayface, and Bane stood behind Mr. Freeze. They looked impatient.

"Frozen. Shining. Perfect. A wasteland paradise," said Mr. Freeze. "It's everything I've ever dreamed."

"Cold enough to ditch your freeze suit yet?" asked the Penguin.

"Yes, I think it is," said Mr. Freeze.

He pressed a button on his suit, and it rapidly detached

TARGET AQUIRED

from his body. The heavy armored pieces fell to the ground. Mr. Freeze was now clad in a far less bulky outfit.

"I'm finally free," he said. "I'm glad you were here to see the beginning of this, Oswald. You were instrumental in making it happen."

"Sure, happy to help," replied the Penguin.

Mr. Freeze's lips pulled back into an evil grin, and he said, "But your usefulness has come to an end."

Mr. Freeze reached into his pocket and extracted his freeze ray. He pointed it directly at the Penguin.

"*What?*" cried the Penguin. "But we're partners."

"I'm no fool, Penguin," said Mr. Freeze. "You wanted to return to Gotham City for one reason—to rule it. Now that I *do* rule it, this makes me into your number one enemy."

"Nonsense!" protested the Penguin.

"Perhaps. But that's not a risk I'm willing to take," said Mr. Freeze. "You'll *never* get the upper hand on me, Penguin."

The Penguin chuckled softly.

"Sorry, Victor. But I already have," he said softly. He turned to Bane and Clayface. "Show him, boys," ordered the Penguin.

Bane and Clayface smiled as they each held injectors

against their arms. A purple stew of poisons sloshed within each device. Both villains squeezed their fingers on the plungers of their injectors, and the purple chemicals flowed into their veins.

"No! You *couldn't* have!" cried out Mr. Freeze.

"Oh, but I *did*," replied the Penguin.

Bane rapidly grew wider and taller. His muscles bulged alarmingly. Soon he was over fifty feet tall.

"The power! The strength!" he called out. "This was worth the wait!"

Clayface stood at Bane's side, now mutated to an equal height.

"Nothing can stop me now!" he yelled.

Mr. Freeze turned to the Penguin and angrily said, "You used the formula? Croc was a durable test subject, but the *others*? Do you have any idea how unstable they are?"

"Do you have any idea how *little* I care?" said the Penguin with a shrug. "And without the defenses of your freeze suit, there's nothing you can do to stop me."

"You'll never get away with this!" Mr. Freeze thundered. "I will see that—"

Before he could finish his sentence, Clayface grabbed Mr. Freeze within his giant paw and hurled him into the air. Mr. Freeze landed in a snowdrift over a mile away.

"It looks like you *will* get away with this, Penguin," said Clayface with a chuckle.

The Penguin turned to Bane and Clayface.

"Bring me the Batman!" he commanded. "He'll pay for putting me in exile! And then Gotham City will finally, rightfully, belong to me!"

"You bet," said Clayface as he began to walk away.

Bane followed closely behind. He was muttering to himself, "But first, I've got a score to settle."

City sanitation plows struggled to clear the giant mounds of snow that had formed in front of the Gotham City Public Library. Weary and shivering citizens slowly filed into the building, where a makeshift shelter had been set up. Nightwing and Commissioner Gordon were standing outside the building, when a blur of red suddenly appeared. It was The Flash.

"Hey, Nightwing!" The Flash said with a smile. "Good to see you! You must not be getting my texts."

Nightwing rolled his eyes and muttered, "I got them."

"Oh," The Flash said with confusion. "But—?"

Nightwing turned back to Gordon and said abruptly, "More urgent stuff to deal with right now, Flash!"

*THUD! THUD!*

The ground shook as the giant Killer Croc thundered into view.

*THUD! THUD!*

Just then, Bane emerged from behind a building. He was now almost as tall as Killer Croc.

"Time to settle up, Croc!" Bane called out.

A grin formed on Killer Croc's face as he turned to face Bane.

"Happy to," he snarled.

The two monsters drew back their massive fists and viciously pummeled the other.

*BLAM! BLAM!*

The Flash looked up with a mix of wonder and terror. "Can't say I expected to see that today!"

"Can't say I expected to see *any* of this today," added Nightwing.

"Come on, guys," said Gordon with a sigh. "This *is* Gotham City."

Nightwing reached for his communicator device.

"Batman, it's Nightwing," he said. "It looks like our big problems just got even bigger."

Batman and Robin were standing on a nearby rooftop. The Dark Knight spoke into the communicator in his cowl.

"I have eyes on it too," he said, "We have to shut

them down before Gotham City is destroyed."

Robin glanced down and noticed a deep shadow beginning to form around the Dynamic Duo. With a start, he turned around and saw the looming form of Clayface. The monster's giant fist was heading directly toward them.

"Ooooof!" yelled Batman as Robin threw himself at the Dark Knight. With just seconds to spare, Robin knocked Batman out of the way of Clayface's thundering fist. As the two heroes tumbled to the street, Robin broke their fall by firing a roped Batarang at a nearby wall.

"Good work, Robin!" Batman said, but the moment was short-lived.

*SLAM! SLAM!*

Clayface continued to knock his fists against the nearby buildings, searching for his enemies.

As he came into view, he raised his fists in anger. "There you are!" he thundered.

Suddenly, Clayface paused. A look of pain filled his face, and he started to groan. As Batman and Robin watched in astonishment, fiery red flames appeared within the folds of his spongy brown body. Clayface opened his mouth, and a spray of red-hot lava erupted into the air.

"What's happening to me?" he cried out. "Freeze's formula, it's—it's—"

Another blast of lava shot out of his mouth and melted a nearby snowdrift.

"He's unstable," said Batman. "Whatever Freeze did, Clayface can't handle it. Here."

Batman extended his hand to Robin to offer him a small metal object.

"What's this?" Robin asked.

Batman smiled. "It's the key. You said you wanted to drive the Batmobile."

"I kind of took that back," Robin said nervously.

"I've got a plan," said Batman. "But I need you to buy me time. Try to keep Clayface from destroying the city until I get back."

"That's a pretty tall order."

Batman pressed the key into Robin's hand and said, "I know you can do it."

"You need a ride?" Robin asked.

"I've got one," said Batman. He removed a small device from his Utility Belt and pressed a button. He turned to look behind them.

"Um, is your ride . . . invisible?" Robin asked doubtfully.

"Wait for it," replied Batman.

*ROOOOOAR!*

A sleek and shiny Batcycle sped down the street toward them. It stopped directly in front of Batman.

"A new Batcycle?" Robin said. *"Nice!"*

Batman jumped onto the Batcycle and pumped the accelerator handle.

"Can you show me how to get the spikes to work on the Batmobile tires before you—?" Robin began.

Before he could finish his question, Batman had zoomed away.

"He does that to everyone, doesn't he?" Robin said to himself.

Robin's thoughts were interrupted by the thundering sound of Clayface behind him. The monster was now alight with bright red flames shooting out of his body.

"Even better!" Clayface bellowed. "Instead of crushing you, now I'll *burn you*!"

Robin hopped into the Batmobile and studied the video screens and the dozens of buttons on the dashboard.

"Okay, what does Batman usually do?" Robin said. He tentatively pushed one button. "This is the ignition, right?"

*VROOOOM!*

Rocket flares shot out of the back of the Batmobile, and the vehicle zoomed down the street. Seconds later

Clayface's fiery fist slammed onto the street where the Batmobile had stood.

"Whoooooo-hooooo!" cried out Robin as the Batmobile roared through downtown Gotham City.

"Can't run from me!" called out Clayface in hot pursuit. *BLAM! BLAM! BLAM!*

Clayface's lava-fueled fists smashed into mounds of snow and nearby buildings as he attempted to crush the Batmobile. Robin expertly navigated the vehicle to avoid the monster's blows.

"I don't know what I was worried about," Robin said happily. "This is awesome!"

The Batmobile swung around one icy corner and sped down an alley. Robin looked up in fright and saw a giant brick wall looming in front of him. The Batmobile was heading directly toward the wall.

"Whoa! Whoa! *Whoooooooooa!*" Robin cried out. He desperately punched buttons on the dashboard. "How did Batman do plane mode?! Plane mode *now*!"

One button had the desired effect. Scalloped wings shot out of the Batmobile, and the vehicle instantly trans-formed into the Batwing. The craft now soared straight up into the air, narrowly avoiding the brick wall.

"*Oh yeah!*" sighed Robin.

The hero changed course in the Batwing, piloting the craft directly toward Clayface.

"Eat missiles, lava breath!" called out Robin.

*BLAM! BLAM! BLAM!*

A barrage of missiles bombarded Clayface. With a fiery grin, the monster easily swatted them away.

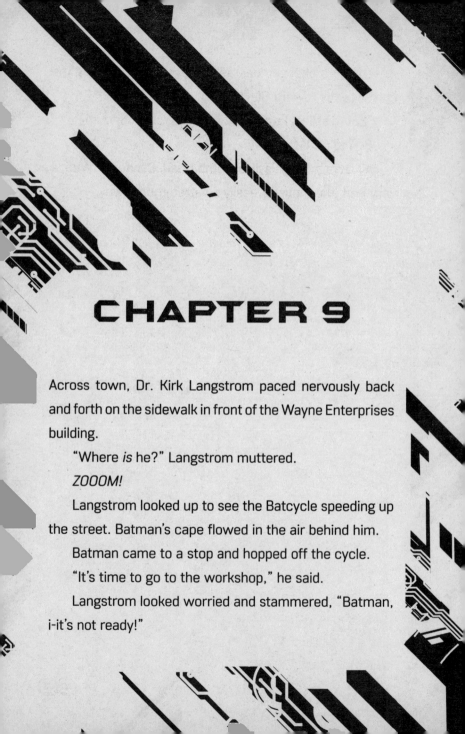

# CHAPTER 9

Across town, Dr. Kirk Langstrom paced nervously back and forth on the sidewalk in front of the Wayne Enterprises building.

"Where *is* he?" Langstrom muttered.

*ZOOOM!*

Langstrom looked up to see the Batcycle speeding up the street. Batman's cape flowed in the air behind him.

Batman came to a stop and hopped off the cycle.

"It's time to go to the workshop," he said.

Langstrom looked worried and stammered, "Batman, i-it's not ready!"

"Giant monsters are loose in Gotham," Batman said gruffly. "Consider this a field test."

Suddenly, an arrow shot through the air and lodged in the entrance to Wayne Enterprises.

"Don't start without me!" Green Arrow called out, joining his allies.

"*There* you are," said a relieved Langstrom.

"What are *you* doing here?" asked Batman.

"You'll see," said Green Arrow. The three men entered the building.

Langstrom turned to Batman and said, "I'm concerned that the magnetometer might be miscalibrated."

"That won't be a problem," replied Batman.

"But, Batman!" protested Langstrom. "You don't understand. Some of the servos are registering at suboptimal PSI ratings."

"Doctor, I've seen the specs. I can handle it."

Langstrom reached up to touch a holographic panel on the wall. He punched in a security code, and a giant metal door opened in front of them.

"This way," he said, leading Batman and Green Arrow down a long, dark hallway.

At the end of the hallway, Langstrom touched a button to illuminate a large room. Green Arrow gasped when he viewed the giant robot standing before them. It was over one hundred feet tall and looked like a giant robotic version of the Dark Knight. A giant bat emblem filled its metallic chest, and sharp gauntlets appeared at the sides of its robotic wrists.

"A Bat-Mech!" said Green Arrow with admiration. "Nice!"

"Boot it up," said Batman.

Langstrom sighed and walked over to a bank of computers. He reluctantly pushed a series of buttons. As he did that, a mechanical hum filled the room, and the platform beneath them began to rise. It went all the way up to the head of the Bat-Mech. A bright yellow light glowed within the device's eye sockets.

Green Arrow turned to Langstrom and asked, "Um, did you forget something?"

Langstrom looked embarrassed and quickly said, "Oh, of course."

He pushed a different series of buttons on the computer. Across the room another device sprang to life. It was a giant Green Arrow robot, as large as the Bat-Mech. One of this robot's mechanical hands clasped a large energy crossbow weapon.

"I think that'll do," said Green Arrow with a smile.

"You ordered your own mech?" Batman asked.

"You think you're the *only* billionaire in the world?" replied Green Arrow. "I convinced Langstrom that you might need some backup."

Langstrom looked away and mumbled, "You see, the Queen Industries contract helped support research and development. We filed a report. . . ."

Batman ignored him and climbed over the scaffold lift. He hopped onto the Bat-Mech's shoulder and then into a chair behind the head that lowered into the cockpit.

"Let's go," he said.

Within the cockpit, a mechanical voice intoned, "Welcome, Batman."

Batman took hold of the controls in the cockpit. "Prepare to deploy."

At his computer, Langstrom said, "Copy that. Actuator systems . . . nominal."

Langstrom pushed a button, and lights began to flash on the Bat-Mech.

"E-systems . . . one hundred percent," Langstrom called out. "Weapons systems . . . online."

The Bat-Mech raised its arm. Its giant mechanical fist opened and then clenched tight.

Langstrom intoned, "Launch in ten, nine, eight, seven, six, five, four, three, two, one."

A roof panel opened above the Bat-Mech.

Batman grasped the robot's control devices and said, "Launch!"

*BLAM!*

A blast of flames erupted from the Bat-Mech's outstretched metal wings. The giant robot shot through the roof and soared into the nighttime sky above Gotham City.

"Hey, wait for me!" called out Green Arrow as he clambered into the cockpit of the Arrow-Mech.

Seconds later the two giant robots were flying past Gotham City's tallest skyscrapers.

"This is one sweet ride!" Green Arrow said happily.

Batman spoke into his communicator device and said, "Green Arrow, you're on Chemo. Stop the freezing process."

"My pleasure," said Green Arrow as he diverted his mech toward the harbor.

"Langstrom, I need something else from you," said Batman.

Langstrom gulped and said nervously, "You do?"

In the middle of downtown Gotham City, Bane and Killer Croc were still engaged in hand-to-hand combat. Each villain was determined to conquer the other, and both were oblivious to the massive damage they were causing.

*KER-BLAM!*

Bane punched Croc in the stomach and pushed the scaly giant against a building. Half the building crumbled, sending broken glass and steel beams falling to the ground, where pedestrians ran in terror.

Killer Croc jumped to his feet, spun around, and whipped his tail behind him. *SMACK!*

Croc's tail lashed into Bane's face and knocked the giant to the ground. Bane groaned in pain.

"Masked freak: zero! Croc: *everything*!" yelled Killer Croc.

A large screen atop a nearby skyscraper caught Croc's attention. A newscaster on the screen was reading a report.

"We can now confirm that the mysterious freezing conditions falling over Gotham City are a result of an attack by super-villains believed to be connected to the sightings of giant monsters roaming the streets—" she said.

Killer Croc smiled and pulled back his fist.

*SMASH!*

With one quick move, Croc shattered the screen into tiny fragments.

The Flash, Nightwing, and Commissioner Gordon were standing nearby, watching the destruction with dismay.

"Aw, come on! That was my favorite TV!" complained The Flash.

Suddenly, all three men looked up in surprise to see the giant Bat-Mech zooming into view.

"Whoa! Is that Batman?" asked The Flash.

Nightwing shook his head and said, "You know, your mouth runs faster than your brain, speedster. Who *else* would that be?"

The Bat-Mech landed in front of Killer Croc with a *thud*. The giant villain grinned in anticipation.

Across town, Robin piloted the Batwing so that it flew circles around the lava-spewing Clayface.

"What does this button do?" wondered Robin as he pressed a red button on the dashboard.

*ZAP! ZAP! ZAP!*

Bright yellow lasers shot out of the Batwing and bombarded Clayface. The villain screamed in pain and slowly dissolved into a huge, gooey mass of red-hot lava.

"Oh yeah!" yelled Robin happily as he flew over the remains of Clayface.

Robin's smile faded rapidly, though, as he watched Clayface rebuild his body. Soon the monster was once again a giant oozing mass of lava-infused clay.

"*Nothing* is stopping this guy!" groaned Robin.

Clayface stretched one of his lava arms directly toward the Batwing. "I've got you, Boy Wonder!" he called out.

"It's impossible to stop me!" taunted Robin.

Seconds later the lava wrapped around one of the wings of the craft. Robin twisted the Batwing's steering device, but the vehicle spun wildly out of control.

The Batwing plummeted toward the ground. "And by *impossible*, obviously I meant *totally possible*!" Robin admitted.

"Which one was it again?!" he yelled as he frantically pushed buttons on the dashboard.

The Batwing slammed into the ground just as Robin pushed the correct button. The vehicle instantly transformed back into the Batmobile and skidded to a stop on the icy road.

"Had it under control the whole time," Robin said with a very relieved sigh.

In the distance Robin saw Clayface slowly moving away in search of the hero, smashing his fist against an elevated subway track. The metal structure crumbled to the ground from the impact.

Robin muttered to himself, "Batman says, 'Keep

Clayface from destroying the whole city.' *Sure. No problem!*"

A voice on his communicator device interrupted him.

"Robin, come in!"

"Dr. Langstrom, is that you?" asked Robin.

"Yes, Batman sent me. I'm headed your way, fast," said Langstrom. "Um . . . *too fast!*"

Robin looked up and saw a Bat-ATV barreling down the street. Dr. Langstrom was perched uneasily on the vehicle, trying to slow its progress. The ATV skidded to an abrupt stop next to the Batmobile.

"This vehicle travels *far* too fast!" Langstrom said, and clambered out of the seat.

"Yeah, it's *awesome*," agreed Robin. "What have you got?"

Langstrom spread a big set of blueprints over the hood of the Batmobile. On them were a series of charts and technical schematics.

"Batman has a plan for dealing with the lava creature," said Langstrom as he perused the papers. "But it's only at the design stage."

The Arrow-Mech floated at the edge of Gotham Harbor. Chemo was still standing in the bay. One arm was sucking in water and the other was spewing out an arctic spray of snow and ice.

Green Arrow called out, "Hey, Chemo. The kids of Gotham City are happy to build snow forts and have snowball fights in the summer. But enough's enough."

Chemo barely glanced at the Arrow-Mech.

"Hello? I'm talking to you!" said Green Arrow.

The hero pulled a lever inside the cockpit, and the Arrow-Mech raised one of its arms. An energy crossbow glowed at the end of the mech's hand. Green Arrow drew back the bow and fired a series of laser blasts directly at Chemo. The monster reeled from the impact and sank into the water.

Seconds later Chemo resurfaced and resumed spraying ice over Gotham City.

"Okay, *now* you're just hurting my feelings," said Green Arrow with a frown.

The Arrow-Mech lunged forward, running up to Chemo.

*BLAM!*

The fist of the Arrow-Mech slammed up against the monster. With a roar, the giant villain emerged from the harbor and sprayed an arctic blast at the Arrow-Mech, knocking it off-balance.

As Green Arrow struggled to restore the Arrow-Mech's balance, Chemo continued to bombard the device with a spray of ice and snow. Soon the mech was unable to move its arms or legs.

Inside the cockpit of the Arrow-Mech, bright red warning lights were flashing, warning of a circuit overload. Green Arrow struggled at the control panel, trying to force the mech to raise its right arm. Finally, Green Arrow succeeded, and a blast of laser energy shot out of the mech. Chemo tumbled backward momentarily, giving Green Arrow just enough time to shake the ice off his mech suit.

"Let's try that again," Green Arrow said. The villain shook off Mr. Freeze's now-damaged arctic device and collided with the Arrow-Mech in the water, sending a giant wave onto the shore.

In the middle of downtown Gotham City, the Penguin and Buzz peered through a window on the top floor of a dark skyscraper. It was the Aviary, the tallest building in Gotham City, which the Penguin had owned before his exile to Antarctica. Now the villain and his companion surveyed the similarly icy, deserted streets below them.

"Which building do you want, Buzz?" asked the Penguin. "You can have your pick."

A suspicious voice called out, "Who's there?"

The Penguin spun around and confronted a nervous man wearing a uniform. It was the building's security guard, and he looked surprised.

"Mister Cobblepot. You're back, sir," said the guard. "We haven't seen you for some time."

"You're going to be seeing a lot more of me now," the Penguin said with a chuckle. "Care to know why?"

The Penguin paused dramatically and then said, "Because Gotham City belongs to *me* now! And not even Batman can do anything about it!"

The Penguin cackled with delight and held up Buzz in front of the guard.

"Oh yes," he continued. "And meet my right-hand penguin, Buzz. I'm naming him head of security."

"Uh . . . n-nice to meet you, uh, boss," the guard stammered as he shook Buzz's flipper awkwardly.

The Penguin and Buzz slowly made their way out of the penthouse. The guard shook his head and muttered, "Yeah, I think it's about time for me to *retire*!"

# CHAPTER 10

Chilly winds swept through the air as two men huddled together on the rooftop of the Gotham City Police Department building. Dr. Langstrom pointed to a large piece of paper in his hand that showed a series of schematic drawings. Nightwing studied the paper intently.

"In theory, it will be the most powerful laser cannon ever constructed," said Langstrom.

The two men looked up to observe Robin perched on top of a large pile of gears and metal parts. Robin was tightening a socket with one hand and consulting a set of instructions in the other hand. The young hero looked confused.

"In theory," repeated Dr. Langstrom with a worried look on his face.

"Don't worry," called out Robin. "I'm sure we can get this laser cannon going in . . . *ouch!*"

A white-hot spark shot out of the device, causing Robin to cry out in pain and drop the wrench. Dr. Langstrom handed it to him with an apologetic look.

"This should pull in enough amps," Nightwing said as he hauled a thick electrical cable over to the laser cannon.

*ZIIIIP!*

The Flash suddenly appeared on the rooftop. He was carrying two large metallic devices in his hands.

"Okay, that's most of the stuff," he said.

"What took so long?" asked Nightwing. "You've been gone for, like, two full minutes."

The Flash grinned with embarrassment and said, "Some of the things on the list were only available in Central City."

"Excuses, excuses," muttered Nightwing.

The Flash disappeared in a blur of red and called out, "Be right back. I'll go get the rest of it."

Robin climbed down from the laser cannon and said, "So, Dr. Langstrom. This cannon will be powerful enough to cut Clayface down to size?"

"Batman hopes so," Langstrom replied.

"Great! Wait . . . *hopes*?" Robin asked quickly. "He doesn't *know*?"

"Well, the last time a giant lava monster attacked Gotham City was . . . *never*," Langstrom said with a frown. "So, no, we haven't had a lot of chances to test it out."

Unnoticed by Langstrom and the heroes, a solitary figure was standing on a nearby rooftop, observing their progress.

It was Mr. Freeze.

Across town, the giant Killer Croc was striding down a deserted street. He drove his fist into the brick wall of an apartment building. His tail lashed out behind him, sending automobiles flying down the block.

"It's over, Croc!" called out a voice.

Killer Croc spun around to confront the Bat-Mech, which stood behind him.

"You think some robot is going to stop me?" Croc said with a harsh laugh. "It's just one of your toys!"

Inside the machine, Batman said, "And here's another one."

The Bat-Mech raised its right arm, revealing a rocket-propelled Batarang launcher. The weapon shot through the air and slammed into Killer Croc's jaw.

Croc was knocked off-balance, and the Bat-Mech

quickly marched over to Croc and started pummeling the giant monster with its mechanical fists.

"I'll break your machine, Batman!" yelled the villain. He opened his mouth to reveal sharp fangs.

*CHOMP!*

Killer Croc's mouth tightened around the Bat-Mech's arm. Batman struggled to free the robot's arm, but Croc was too strong. The scaly monster knocked the machine against a nearby building. Bricks and broken glass fell on top of the Bat-Mech.

Just then, Batman looked up to see an even more dangerous menace moving toward him. It was the giant Bane. Croc landed a hard punch, and the Bat-Mech went stumbling backward . . .

Right into the arms of Bane.

With an evil laugh, Bane easily lifted the Bat-Mech and trapped the robot within his giant, muscled arms. Killer Croc smiled and moved closer to them. While Bane held the Bat-Mech in place, Croc threw powerful punches at the machine. Croc then snapped his tail in the air and delivered a crushing blow against his opponent.

Bane gripped the Bat-Mech even tighter and bellowed, "I'm going to pry open that shell of yours, Batman . . . so I can get to the soft center!"

Holding the Bat-Mech within one giant arm, Bane reached up to peel off a metal panel at the back of the machine. Underneath the panel was an array of six laser cannons. All six were pointed directly at Bane.

"What the—" began the villain.

*BLAM!*

All six cannons fired at Bane. The giant villain was knocked to the ground.

Batman quickly turned his attention back to Killer Croc.

The monster's claws were fully extended as he lunged at the mech. Inside the device, Batman pulled the control levers, raising the Bat-Mech's arms and delivering one powerful blow after another to Croc. Each time Killer Croc fell to the ground, though, he jumped back to his feet and attacked the Bat-Mech.

With a roar, Killer Croc ran toward the Bat-Mech and collided against the machine. Batman struggled inside the cockpit to control the mech's arms. While Croc pummeled the machine with his deadly fists, Batman managed to grasp Croc with the mech's arms and lift the giant villain up into the air.

The startled monster tumbled backward, which gave Batman an opportunity to grab Croc's tail. The Bat-Mech swung the monster in the air, looping him around higher and higher. Finally, the Bat-Mech threw Killer Croc to the ground. The impact knocked him out. The unconscious monster slowly shrank down to his normal size as Mr. Freeze's serum wore off.

*SMASH!*

Bane's massive fist slammed into the Bat-Mech. The machine was knocked to its knees. As Batman struggled to raise the mech to its feet, Bane loomed over the machine. With an evil smile, Bane lifted his foot and kicked the Bat-Mech with all his strength. The impact of the blow caused the Bat-Mech to topple backward and fall over. A hiss of smoke arose from the machine as its electrical circuits began to overload. The yellow lights within the Bat-Mech's cowl slowly faded to black.

"Thank you for doing my dirty work, Batman," called out Bane. "With Killer Croc out of the way, I'll be able to enjoy my dominion over Gotham City."

Inside the Bat-Mech, Batman glanced down at the control panel.

*System overload. Shutting down,* was the message that appeared on a video screen.

Batman called out to Bane and asked, "You plan to dominate Gotham City as the Penguin's flunky?"

Bane glared at the machine and said, "The Penguin is a means to an end."

"Looks to me like he's sitting back and watching you do all the work," taunted Batman as he reached over to press a series of buttons on the mech's control panel.

"Tell me, Batman," Bane said. He grasped the cowl of the Bat-Mech and lifted the device into the air. "Between Penguin and me, *who is the bigger man*?" Bane drew back his thickly muscled arm, ready to deliver a fatal blow to the Bat-Mech.

Batman smiled as the Bat-Mech's video screen displayed the message, *Starting up . . .*

"Don't forget what they say about 'the bigger they are,'" said Batman, quickly swinging a mechanical arm toward Bane.

*KER-BLAM!*

The Bat-Mech's mechanical fist collided with Bane's giant hand. Bane grunted in pain from the impact. Batman struggled within the Bat-Mech to overpower the villain.

Bane's face contorted with anger as the Bat-Mech closed its grasp around Bane's giant hand. As the villain staggered backward, Batman raised the Bat-Mech's other arm to deliver a powerful blow. Bane was thrown to the ground with a loud thud.

At the edge of the Gotham Harbor, the battle continued between Green Arrow and Chemo. The monster reached out its giant arms to grasp the Arrow-Mech and tossed the device into the air. The mech landed with a crash on the icy shore.

Inside the Arrow-Mech, Green Arrow muttered, "This day at the beach is turning out to be no day at the beach!"

Chemo stretched out his arms and smashed a nearby wharf. The monster was moving closer to the Arrow-Mech. Green Arrow quickly moved the device away from the shore and toward the buildings at the edge of the water.

"Computer, are all of these buildings evacuated?" he quickly asked.

"Affirmative, no life signs detected," replied the mech's computer.

"Show me which ones I own," Green Arrow said.

Four nearby buildings appeared on a video screen, and the computer voice said, "Displaying now."

"Oh, good," Green Arrow said with a relieved sigh. "Because I have *great* insurance."

Green Arrow pivoted the mech around and charged directly at Chemo. The mech grabbed Chemo and lifted the monster in its robotic arms. It then hurled Chemo directly toward a Queen Industries building.

*SMASH!*

The monster crashed through the building's entrance and tumbled inside. Chemo was quickly buried beneath a mountain of twisted steel and granite.

"Well, that building needed a renovation anyway," said Green Arrow.

Across town, on the roof of the Gotham City Police Department building, Dr. Langstrom peered anxiously at the completed laser cannon. Standing next to him were The Flash, Nightwing, and Robin.

"You're sure it's ready to be tested?" asked Nightwing.

"I'm afraid we don't have time to work up a better prototype," replied Langstrom.

He nodded at the heroes and pressed a button on a small device in his hands. The laser cannon came to life and emitted a low mechanical hum. Soon, the entire machine started to glow.

"That's a good sign," observed Robin.

A bright yellow ray surrounded the machine. Dr. Langstrom and the heroes shielded their eyes. Then the rooftop began to shake.

*BRRRRRRIP!*

Suddenly, the laser cannon gave a violent shudder and stopped moving. A dark cloud of smoke billowed out of the machine.

"And *that's* a bad sign," said Robin.

Langstrom sighed and said, "Batman is *not* going to be happy."

A deep voice startled the four men on the roof.

"The contrivance wouldn't have worked anyway," it said.

Langstrom and the heroes spun around to see Mr. Freeze standing at the edge of the roof.

The Flash sped over to Mr. Freeze and grabbed the villain's arms.

Nightwing angrily asked, "What did you do to the laser cannon?"

"Nothing," Mr. Freeze replied. "The design was flawed. It couldn't support valence cosharing between the bonded particles."

Langstrom looked up from a set of blueprints and said, "He's right. I should have thought of that."

Langstrom sheepishly added, "No one tell Batman, okay?"

Nightwing moved closer to Mr. Freeze and asked,

"Why are you here? We *know* it was you who put Gotham City in a deep freeze."

"It was," Mr. Freeze said sadly. "But I was foolish."

"You're here to turn yourself in?" asked a surprised Nightwing.

Mr. Freeze shook his head and said quietly, "No, I'm here to help."

The Flash rolled his eyes and said, "As if. We're not getting fooled by that old trick!"

The Flash walked over to the other heroes and asked doubtfully, "Are we?"

"Why would you want to help us clean up your mess, Freeze?" asked Robin.

"Precisely for that reason," replied Mr. Freeze. "Because it is *my* mess. All I wanted was to be left alone in my desolate land. But Penguin convinced me to assault Gotham City. I was manipulated . . . and then betrayed."

"You're not going to get away by blaming this on other people," said Nightwing.

"No, I will take responsibility for my actions," said Mr. Freeze. "Penguin's betrayal made me realize what I was doing to Gotham City. How can I expect to be left alone to live my life, if I do not leave others alone to live theirs?"

"I'll admit, that made sense," said Nightwing.

The Flash frowned and said, "Really? Are you kidding? Because all I'm hearing is *I'mabadguy. I'mabadguy. I'mabadguy.*"

Nightwing ignored The Flash and continued to study Mr. Freeze's face.

"You said something about helping?" asked Robin.

Mr. Freeze reached into a pocket of his outfit, which caused all three heroes to spring into action. Nightwing drew his eskrima sticks. The Flash zoomed closer to Mr. Freeze.

Mr. Freeze sighed with irritation and slowly withdrew his three-pronged arctic device from his pocket. It was identical to the one that had created the giant Killer Croc.

"This is one of my arctic devices," said Mr. Freeze. "Coupled with your cannon, it could be an effective weapon against Clayface."

"But what is—?" Langstrom asked as Mr. Freeze handed him the arctic device. "Oh, I see. Brilliant."

Langstrom turned to the three heroes and said, "Freeze is right. It could work. But he would have to help us set it up."

Robin turned to the other heroes and said, "Then, the question is, can we trust him?"

"No," The Flash said quickly.

Nightwing seemed doubtful as he peered into Mr. Freeze's face.

"Maybe . . ." said Nightwing.

"I better call the boss on this one," said Robin.

# CHAPTER 11

At the northern edge of Gotham City, the battle continued to rage between Batman and Bane.

Batman swung the Bat-Mech's mechanical arm in the air and landed a heavy blow against Bane. The giant villain fell to the ground, shattering the icy street below him. Bane quickly jumped to his feet and charged toward the Bat-Mech. Bane reached out his mighty arms and pulled the Bat-Mech toward him. The mech was trapped against Bane's massive chest, unable to escape.

"Your mech has a back!" bellowed Bane. "I bet I can *break* it!"

Within the cockpit, Batman struggled with the controls, desperately trying to free the mech from Bane's fatal grasp. Batman swung the mech's arms in a circular motion, knocking Bane off-balance. The Bat-Mech's two metallic fists smashed into Bane's head. The villain grunted in pain and crumpled to the ground.

Suddenly, an image of Robin appeared on the screen inside the Bat-Mech's cockpit. Batman continued to pilot the mech as he listened to Robin.

"I need advice," said Robin. "Langstrom's laser is a bust, but Mr. Freeze is here, and he says that he can get it to work."

"Do it," instructed Batman.

"You think we can *trust* him?" asked Robin.

Bane jumped to his feet and grasped the Bat-Mech. With a loud grunt, the villain lifted the Bat-Mech and hurled it down the street. The Bat-Mech crashed into an elevated subway track. The impact cut the track in two, and debris from the wreckage tumbled to the streets.

"Imagine being partners with the Penguin," said Batman. He was struggling to bring the Bat-Mech to its feet.

"I'd rather not," Robin replied.

Bane was moving closer to the Bat-Mech. The villain

picked up a large piece of metal debris from the train track. He hoisted it in his hand and swung it menacingly.

"Working with the Penguin is an easy thing to regret," said Batman. "Victor's whole personality is built on *guilt*. He's got enough of a conscience to want to make amends."

"Got it. Robin out."

The holographic image disappeared, and Batman turned his attention back to Bane.

*CRASH!*

Bane smashed the metal wreckage against the Bat-Mech. Batman returned a counterpunch that slammed into Bane's stomach.

Bane smiled as he noticed a large gas truck parked on the street near him. The truck was marked with large FLAMMABLE warning signs. The giant villain reached down and easily lifted the truck off the street like a toy. With all his strength, he threw the truck at the Bat-Mech.

*BLAM!*

A fireball of combustible gas erupted in the air as the truck smashed into the Bat-Mech. Smoke poured from the mech as it fell to the ground, but it was still intact. Bane jumped high in the air, arms outstretched and ready to land on top of the Bat-Mech. Batman raised the mech's arms, which quickly caught Bane and then threw the villain against a building. Almost immediately, Bane jumped to his feet and started running toward the Bat-Mech.

Inside the cockpit Batman quickly pressed a red button on the control panel. The rocket-powered Batarang emerged once more from the mech's left arm. A bright blast of flames erupted from the back of the device, and it went soaring through the air, flying directly toward Bane.

*WHOOSH!*

Bane reached out one giant hand to swat away the weapon, but the missile found its target and sliced through one of the heavy-duty tubes that supplied the poisonous Venom solution to Bane. Mr. Freeze's serum flowed from the tube, splattering the white snow with purple liquid.

Bane attempted to stop the flow by pinching the tube shut with his fingers. He rolled his other hand into a fist and tried to punch the Bat-Mech. But Batman was too fast for him. The Bat-Mech jumped out of the way and brought one of its mechanical hands down on top of Bane's head. Another punch from the Bat-Mech slammed into the villain's stomach.

*WHOOSH!*

Batman launched another massive Batarang, but this one had a thick metal cable attached to it. The Batarang looped around Bane, tightly binding him with the cable. As the villain struggled to free himself, the Bat-Mech gave a sharp tug on the cable. Bane flew through the air toward the Bat-Mech. With a grim smile, Batman raised one of the Bat-Mech's arms and formed a fist.

*KER-BLAM!*

The Bat-Mech's fist collided against Bane's face.

Bane cried out in agony and fell on his back. As the last of Freeze's serum spurted from the tube, Bane began to decrease in size. Soon, he was back to his original size, sprawled on the snowy street.

Ten feet away, still unconscious and buried in a mound of snow, was Killer Croc.

Commissioner Gordon and two police officers moved tentatively toward the two villains.

"Well, well, well," said Commissioner Gordon. He surveyed the scene with a smile. "We have Batman to thank for . . ."

Before he could finish his sentence, he looked up to see the Bat-Mech walking away. It was heading toward the harbor.

The Arrow-Mech stood at the edge of Gotham Harbor. Inside the device, Green Arrow studied the wreckage of his Queen Industries building. The entrance to the building was in ruins, and there was no sign of Chemo.

"Huh. Who knew that's all it would take?" said Green Arrow with a contented smile.

Green Arrow piloted the mech through the wreckage and stepped inside the building.

"Reveal any life forms," he commanded the mech.

The video screen before him began to hum. It displayed the message *Analyzing* as it scanned the interior of the building.

Green Arrow frowned as the message changed to *Anomaly found*. The video screen revealed a green mass, slowly moving within the wreckage. It was Chemo!

The monster opened its mouth wide and launched a deadly blast of bright green acid toward the Arrow-Mech. Green Arrow quickly moved the mech out of the way, but the acid slammed into two support columns in the middle of the room. The columns disintegrated from the impact of the acid, causing the roof to shatter.

"Oh no," said Green Arrow. The building began crumbling into pieces.

Green Arrow moved to pilot the mech out of the building, but he wasn't fast enough. With a loud crash, the entire structure collapsed. A huge cloud of smoke and flying debris filled the air.

Seconds later a dusty and dented mechanical hand

emerged from the rubble. It was the Arrow-Mech, painfully crawling from the wreckage.

"Me and my big external speaker," groaned Green Arrow.

*WHOOOSH!*

Chemo launched himself into the air. He was spewing smoking-hot acid from his mouth, spraying it directly at the Arrow-Mech. Some of the acid splashed onto the Arrow-Mech's right shoulder. The metal in that area sizzled and smoked from the goo.

"Did anyone ever tell you that your power is kind of gross?" asked Green Arrow. He quickly pivoted the Arrow-Mech out of the way.

Chemo didn't respond and moved closer to the hero. Green Arrow pulled back the mech's right arm and delivered a powerful punch to the villain.

*CRUNCH!*

Green Arrow watched in horror as the right arm of the mech came loose and tumbled to the ground. Electrical sparks filled the cockpit of the mech, and the now unbalanced device fell backward, cracking its right leg in the process. As Chemo moved closer, Green Arrow struggled to bring the mech to its feet again.

"Fine," said a nervous Green Arrow. "How about we call it a draw?"

Sizzling hot acid dripped from Chemo's mouth as he reached for the Arrow-Mech. Just as Chemo was about to grasp the mech, a large metallic hand grasped the villain's shoulder. It was the Bat-Mech!

Chemo spun around and opened his mouth. Just inches away from the Bat-Mech, the villain was about to spew forth a stream of metal-eating acid.

*KER-BLAM!*

The Bat-Mech's powerful metal fist smashed into the giant monster. Chemo doubled over in pain. The Bat-Mech reached out to grab the villain and launched him into the air. Chemo sailed across the wreckage and landed with a *thud* against the rubble of the building.

Batman moved the Bat-Mech cautiously toward the monster. Was the battle finally over?

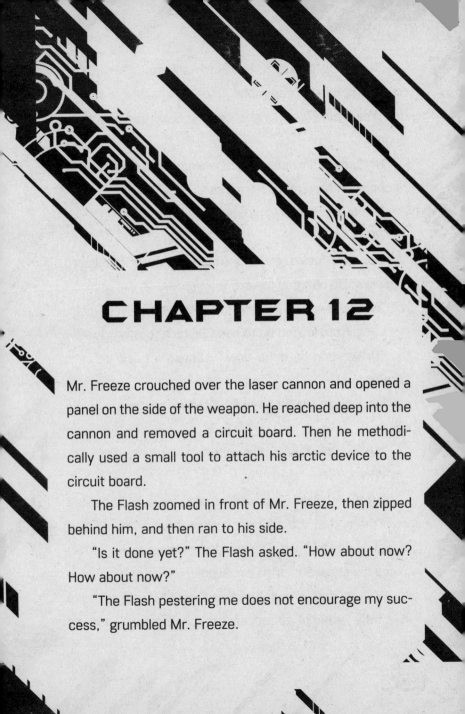

# CHAPTER 12

Mr. Freeze crouched over the laser cannon and opened a panel on the side of the weapon. He reached deep into the cannon and removed a circuit board. Then he methodically used a small tool to attach his arctic device to the circuit board.

The Flash zoomed in front of Mr. Freeze, then zipped behind him, and then ran to his side.

"Is it done yet?" The Flash asked. "How about now? How about now?"

"The Flash pestering me does not encourage my success," grumbled Mr. Freeze.

Nightwing glared at The Flash and said, "So we do have *something* in common!"

"Yeah, but Flash is right," said Robin. "You need to be done."

Dr. Langstrom consulted his holographic control panel to check on Mr. Freeze's progress.

"Done in one more minute," said Langstrom.

*ROAAAAR!*

The lava-fueled giant Clayface suddenly thundered into view. He charged toward the heroes.

"Not sure you've got one more minute!" yelled Robin.

Langstrom looked up to see Clayface moving closer.

"Or we can be done now," Langstrom said quickly. "Now's fine!"

Mr. Freeze calmly pressed a button at the top of the cannon.

"And . . . *fire!*" he commanded.

*WHOOOSH!*

A freezing blast of concentrated snow and ice blasted from the end of the cannon. It shot through the air and crashed into Clayface. The startled monster looked down to see his chest and arms encased in ice.

With an irate growl, Clayface flexed his arm muscles in a futile attempt to loosen the ice. He then stopped struggling as an evil smile filled his face. Clayface's head began to shudder violently. Suddenly, a gusher of red-hot lava erupted from the top of his head. The fiery liquid shot through the air, headed straight toward Langstrom and the others.

ZIP! ZIP! ZIP!

The Flash quickly grabbed Langstrom, Nightwing, and Robin in his arms. He pulled them to safety just as the blast of molten lava hit the rooftop.

Clayface inhaled deeply and flexed his arms again. This time he succeeded in cracking the ice that covered him. He freed his lava-fueled arms and started walking toward the rooftop.

Mr. Freeze was standing on top of the cannon. "The arctic cannon worked briefly," he called out. "But we need a sustained blast!"

WHOMP!

Clayface hurled a handful of red-hot lava toward the roof. It landed next to the cannon. The heat from the lava drifted upward, causing Mr. Freeze to almost fall from the cannon.

"The heat—must not falter . . ." he said with a groan.

Hugging the cannon to support his body, Mr. Freeze touched his hand to the control panel.

*WHOOOSH!*

A massive stream of ice and snow erupted from the cannon. It sailed through the air, heading directly toward Clayface. The monster stood his ground and launched a spray of boiling-hot lava. The ice and lava collided together midair for a few seconds, but the arctic blast was no match for Clayface's lava. The cannon sputtered and went dark. Bursts of lava bombarded the heroes, causing fires to break out on the rooftop. Mr. Freeze closed his eyes in pain as the fires drew closer to him.

"Without his freeze suit, these temperatures will kill him!" yelled Nightwing.

Mr. Freeze swayed on top of the cannon, barely able to hold on to the control panel.

Nightwing ran over to the cannon and called out, "Mr. Freeze, let me operate the cannon. Get away from the lava!"

Mr. Freeze shook his head and said, "Only I can manage the arctic device!"

His face contorted in pain, Mr. Freeze pressed his hand against the control panel.

*WHOOSH!*

An even stronger burst of ice and snow shot out of the cannon. The icy mixture covered Clayface's chest and arms. The monster easily flexed his muscles and shattered the ice. Clayface lobbed more blobs of hot lava at the roof. One of them landed inches away from Mr. Freeze.

Mr. Freeze fell to his knees. He held tightly on to the cannon to keep from tumbling to the rooftop. One of his hands continued to press against the control panel.

"How much more can he take?" asked The Flash.

*WHOOSH!*

Another arctic blast sprayed from the cannon. Clayface was standing directly in front of the building. As the ice continued to bombard him, Clayface raised his lava-fueled arms and roared in triumph.

Suddenly, Clayface looked worried. He was unable to move one ice-covered arm. Soon, another arm was also frozen solid. The ice grew thicker and thicker around Clayface's torso. Next, his legs were trapped within the icy mixture. Finally, his head was covered with ice.

Clayface was no longer able to move. He was completely frozen.

The heroes sighed with relief and turned to thank Mr. Freeze. They watched with dismay as Mr. Freeze toppled from the cannon and fell to the rooftop.

Nightwing rushed over to Mr. Freeze and placed a hand on his shoulder. Mr. Freeze was gasping.

"I—I just wanted . . . solitude," he said quietly.

"Your freeze suit!" said Nightwing. "Where is it?"

Mr. Freeze's eyes slowly closed. He stopped moving.

The docks at Gotham Harbor shook violently as the battle between Batman and Chemo resumed. The monster jumped to his feet and shot out one arm to punch the Bat-Mech. In return, Batman launched missiles at the creature. Chemo retracted his arm and shot a spray of green acid directly at the Bat-Mech.

The incapacitated and now one-armed, one-legged Arrow-Mech was still laying at the edge of the rubble. From within the machine, Green Arrow spoke into his communicator.

"Watch out for the acid thing!" Green Arrow said. "Chemo loves to do the acid thing!"

The Bat-Mech grasped Chemo around the waist and hoisted the monster into the air. Chemo landed with a *thud* in the rubble.

*WHOMP!*

Chemo extended one of his arms and crashed it into the mech. The impact almost completely severed the Bat-Mech's left arm at the shoulder. Batman pulled up the controls for the arm and set it to self-destruct.

"What's happening?" called out Green Arrow. "That doesn't sound good!"

Batman piloted the Bat-Mech to lean forward as it shook off and then caught its now detached mechanical left arm using its functional right arm. He swung the mech's severed metallic arm in the air and threw it at Chemo. The impact knocked the monster backward, which gave Batman enough time to move over to the fallen Arrow-Mech.

Inside the cockpit, Batman punched the command *Patch* on the control panel. He then reached over with the Bat-Mech's one operational arm to grab the Arrow-Mech's one remaining arm.

*RIIIIP!*

The Arrow-Mech's left arm was roughly pulled loose.

"Hey! I think I need that!" protested Green Arrow.

*CRUNCH!*

The Bat-Mech smashed the green mechanical arm onto its left shoulder. The Bat-Mech was once again fully functional. Batman turned the mech around, ready to face Chemo.

With a roar, Chemo charged at the Bat-Mech.

The Bat-Mech soared into the air and pointed its new green mechanical arm directly at Chemo. A glowing green energy crossbow weapon appeared at the end of the arm. The bow drew back and fired a blast of green laser energy at Chemo. The impact of the laser caused the monster to fall back into the rubble.

With a surprised look on his face, Chemo reached down to touch his torso. A rupture now appeared in the middle of his stomach. A steady flow of green acid dripped from the hole.

"You cracked him? Whoa! No one's ever cracked him!" called out Green Arrow.

Chemo lumbered to his feet and shot out one arm to grab the Bat-Mech. He slowly pulled the mech closer to him.

Batman took that opportunity to pummel Chemo with the fists of the Bat-Mech.

*BLAM! BLAM! BLAM!*

With each blow, the fissure in Chemo's stomach grew larger.

Green Arrow's face popped up on a video screen inside the Bat-Mech.

"I'm liking what I'm hearing," he said.

"Green Arrow! I'm trying to concentrate!" Batman grunted. "Arrrgh!"

A spray of green acid spewed out of Chemo's mouth.

Batman quickly piloted the machine out of the way, narrowly avoiding the dangerous liquid.

"Oh, sorry!" said Green Arrow. "Let's see if I can help!"

Green Arrow pressed a button inside the cockpit that opened the Arrow-Mech's door. He jumped out of the device.

Chemo and the Bat-Mech were struggling at the shore of the harbor, their arms locked together in combat. The docks of the harbor were strewn with the debris of ruined buildings. Green Arrow jumped from one pile of rubble to another, moving closer to the battle. He climbed atop the highest pile of bricks at the edge of the harbor. From this vantage point, he removed his bow and loaded an arrow into its bowstring.

*ZIP! ZIP! ZIP!*

Green Arrow shot arrow after arrow toward Chemo. Each arrow found its target: the rapidly expanding hole in the middle of the monster.

"Think we *got him*!" called out Green Arrow.

Batman extracted a vacuum containment device from the Bat-Mech's Utility Belt. He shoved the device deep within the hole in Chemo's stomach.

*GLURP!*

The device quickly sucked the acid from Chemo's

body, taking Mr. Freeze's serum with it. The monster was silent as it swayed from side to side.

"Can I talk now?" asked Green Arrow. "Did we win?"

Batman watched as Chemo fell face-down into the snow. Within seconds, the villain had returned to his normal size.

"We won," replied Batman.

# CHAPTER 13

The icy streets of Gotham were eerily quiet and still blanketed in snow. Only one sound disturbed the silence. It was Mr. Freeze's ice tank barreling down the street. The Penguin was driving the vehicle. In the seat next to him sat his loyal friend, Buzz the penguin.

The Penguin was muttering happily.

"Mayor Cobblepot—no," he said. "Governor Cobblepot—no, no. President Cobblepot—*no! Lord* Cobblepot. *That* has a nice ring to it!"

*CRUNCH! CRUNCH! CRUNCH!*

Huge slabs of melting snow and ice began to fall from

the nearby buildings. The Penguin violently turned the steering wheel to avoid being hit by the falling snow.

"*Ack?!*" he squawked as he halted the vehicle in the middle of the street.

"Melting?" he said angrily. "This isn't supposed to be *melting*!"

The Penguin clambered out of the vehicle and angrily waved his umbrella in the air.

"Where are my monsters?" he shouted. "What are they *doing*?"

*THUD! THUD! THUD!*

The sound of heavy footsteps filled the air. The Penguin smiled.

"Ah, here comes one of my monsters now," he said with a satisfied chuckle.

The Penguin's smile turned to a grimace as he saw the Bat-Mech come stomping around the corner.

"*Waugh!*" the Penguin cried out as he quickly hopped into the tank. Buzz frantically pressed the accelerator and sped down the icy street.

It only took a few steps for the Bat-Mech to reach the fleeing vehicle. The mech reached down and easily grasped the ice tank in its mechanical hand. It lifted the vehicle into the air.

"We've stopped them all, Penguin," said Batman. "It's over."

Inside the vehicle, the Penguin cried out in desperation.

"No! No! No! *Curse you, Batman!*" he screamed.

Green Arrow was perched on the shoulder of the Bat-Mech. He leaned forward to speak to the Penguin.

"You should have seen the look on your face when we came around the corner!" he said with a smile. "It was *priceless*!"

The next morning, as the sun rose over Gotham City, children were frolicking in the snow, throwing snowballs and building snow-people. One kid even built a snow-Batman!

Outside the Gotham City Police Department building, Commissioner Gordon stood next to The Flash and Dr. Langstrom. They watched as police officers carried the now normal-size Bane and Killer Croc on stretchers. A waiting police van was parked nearby.

"They'll be fine," Gordon said, "once they wake up back inside a cell in Arkham Asylum."

The men turned their attention to another group of people toting a stretcher. It was Nightwing and a hospital worker, and they were carrying Mr. Freeze.

"Almost there," said Nightwing.

"So . . . very . . . hot . . ." gasped Mr. Freeze.

Suddenly, the Batcycle roared into view. Robin jumped off the vehicle and ran over to Nightwing. He was carrying the freeze suit.

"I found it!" yelled Robin.

Robin reached out to attach the suit to Mr. Freeze's torso.

"Let me help you," said Robin. He clasped the suit into place.

Mr. Freeze's voice seemed to grow stronger as he said, "Thank you."

The Flash turned to Gordon and asked, "What's going to happen to him?"

Gordon frowned and said, "He'll get a trial, and I imagine he'll be back at Arkham with the others."

"But he *saved* us," protested Robin.

Mr. Freeze stood up from the stretcher, now fully outfitted in his freeze suit.

"Yes, but I caused all this as well," he said sadly.

He turned to Robin and said, "It's all right. Perhaps I can request solitary confinement. I might find the peace I've been looking for."

Batman's voice suddenly filled the chilly air. He was escorting the Penguin down the street. The villain's hands were tied behind his back.

"One more," said Batman, shoving the Penguin forward.

"You may have beaten me this time, but once I'm free—" the Penguin squawked.

"Enough," Batman interrupted.

He shoved the Penguin into the police van.

"I'll have the last laugh over all of you," the Penguin said with a sneer. "Especially you, Batman!"

The doors to the police van slammed shut.

Green Arrow joined the group, carrying the struggling Buzz. The tiny creature tried to bite Green Arrow's arm.

"Yikes! Calm down, little fella. What's gotten into this thing?" asked Green Arrow.

An angry voice erupted from inside the police van.

"Buzz is not a *thing*! He's your better!" called out the Penguin. "When I escape again—"

The Penguin's words faded into the distance as the van drove off in the direction of Arkham Asylum.

A half hour later, the van pulled into Arkham's driveway. Two armed guards escorted the sullen Penguin into the institution's arrival area.

The head of Arkham security greeted the Penguin with a smile.

"Welcome back, Penguin," he said. "Do you remember

that hole you guys blew out in our floor? We have good news for you. During labor duty, you get to help with the reconstruction!"

"Fantastic," muttered the Penguin.

*CLANG!*

A heavy iron cell door slammed shut in front of the Penguin. He surveyed his dark cell with disgust.

"Well, well, well . . ."

A high-pitched voice could be heard in the cell next to the Penguin.

"When I vowed to get even, I had no idea it would be this soon!" called out the Joker.

The Penguin turned to face the thick cement wall between them.

"What are you going to do to me, clown?" he taunted. "You're in *that* cell, and I'm in *this* one!"

"Hee-hee-hee," the Joker chuckled.

*CREAK!*

A roughly carved door suddenly opened in the wall between their cells. The Joker stepped through the door and moved closer to the Penguin.

"You were *saying*?" asked the Joker as an evil grin formed on his face.

"Squawk! Squawk! Squawk!"

Buzz protested and struggled mightily as he was carried down a long, dark hallway. A man in a uniform had the tiny penguin tucked securely underneath one arm. Buzz was determined not to go quietly to prison.

*WHOMP!*

Buzz was tossed through a doorway onto a cold hard floor. A heavy metal door clanged shut behind him. Buzz squawked even louder in protest.

"Squeak! Squeak! Squeak!" came a high-pitched voice behind him.

Buzz spun around in surprise and discovered that a female penguin was waddling closer to him. Behind her stood a dozen other penguins. They were peering at Buzz with curiosity.

Buzz looked around to discover that he had landed in the Gotham City Zoo's penguin exhibit. A refreshing pool of ice-cold water stood at the end of the icy floor. A bucket filled with tasty fish stood near the edge of the pool.

At the other side of the pool, a group of children were laughing in delight.

"Look at the pretty new penguin, daddy!" said one happy child. She pointed directly at Buzz.

Buzz moved closer to the other penguins.

"Squawk," he muttered with contentment.

Back at Wayne Enterprises, Dr. Langstrom was pacing in front of the damaged Bat-Mech that stood at the far end of a large room.

"Have to replace the forward actuators," he muttered. "Clearly new struts along the port side. Must examine the structural integrity of the cockpit."

"Okay, it's bad," he said with a sigh. "But it could be worse. I can fix this."

*ZAP! ZAP!*

The sound of electrical sparks filled the air. Dr. Langstrom spun around and stared at the Arrow-Mech that was sprawled on the floor. Both of the mech's arms were missing, and it was covered with dents and deep gashes in its metal body. Thin clouds of black smoke wafted from the holes in the machine.

"Oh no!" cried Dr. Langstrom. He rushed up to the Arrow-Mech and started sobbing. "What did he *do* to you?"

Inside the Batcave the heroes were gathered together in front of the Batcomputer. Batman was hard at work, inputting data from their latest adventure.

"I heard you let the new kid drive the Batmobile," said Nightwing.

"Yes," replied Batman, not looking up.

"I didn't get to do that for years," said Nightwing, with just a touch of jealousy.

Robin glowed with pride as he listened to their conversation.

The Flash walked over and placed his hand on Nightwing's shoulder.

"The northern lights are supposed to be great in Finland tonight, but they start in twenty seconds, so I have to leave soon," said The Flash. "Great working with you again, buddy."

"I'm *not* your buddy," muttered Nightwing.

"Oh, what a kidder!" The Flash called out as he zoomed out of the Batcave.

Alfred offered a cup of tea to Nightwing, but the hero just shook his head and launched a cabled Batarang into the air. Seconds later he was swinging through the air and exiting the Batcave.

Green Arrow yawned and started walking away.

"I'm outta here too," he said. "There's a Queen Industries building down by the harbor that needs some reconstruction. See you when I see you, Bats."

Robin gulped and approached the Dark Knight.

"Batman, I know I haven't been the new Robin for

very long," he said, "but thank you for taking me on this mission. I learned a lot."

Batman stopped typing at the Batcomputer.

"Robin, I . . ." he began. "I owe you. The whole city owes you. We couldn't have done it without your help today."

"Wow, thanks! That means a lot."

Batman turned back to the Batcomputer.

"Hey, I was going to train," said Robin. "Wanna come? You can help me learn how to do those quick getaways you're always pulling."

Batman smiled and said, "Okay. Let's go."

As Batman and Robin walked toward the training room, Batman said, "Alfred, you're on watch duty."

"Of course, sir."

Robin turned to Batman and asked, "Have you *really* been to a whole planet-wide amusement park?

"Yes."

"How was it?" asked Robin, hoping for some exciting details.

"Enjoyable," said Batman.

# CHAPTER 14

The sun was shining in downtown Gotham City, and the ice was steadily melting. Children gathered around the giant frozen remains of Clayface, pelting it with icy snowballs.

*WHOMP! WHOMP! WHOMP!*

Suddenly, a tiny crack appeared in the middle of the ice. As the children continued to throw snowballs, the crack grew wider and wider.

*CRASH!*

The ice surrounding Clayface shattered into pieces and tumbled to the ground. The terrified children started screaming and ran down the street as fast as they could.

There was silence for a few moments.

Then a glob of brown goo formed at the edge of the pile of cracked ice. The brown mass slowly began to increase in size. It grew ever larger and finally formed into the fearsome form of Clayface.

He climbed over the shards of ice and chuckled quietly to himself. An evil grin spread over the monster's face. Seconds later, he slithered into a nearby sewer grate.

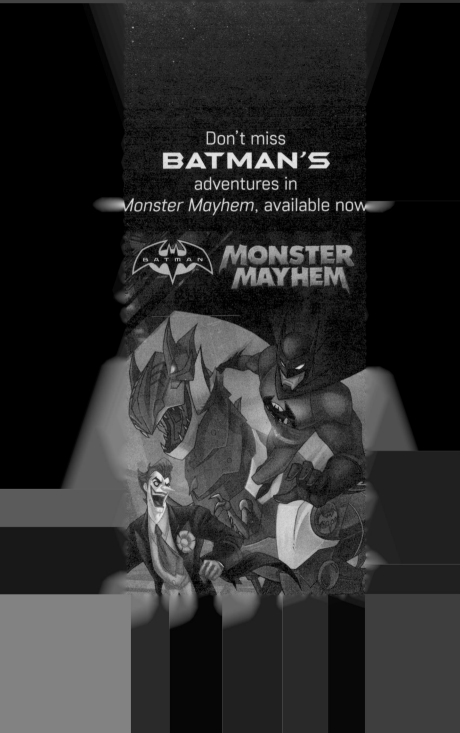

# CHAPTER 1

On the outskirts of Gotham City, high atop a hill, stood the dark and foreboding institution known as Arkham Asylum. It took a special type of criminal to end up at Arkham. Within the asylum's walls were some of the most dangerous foes ever to fight Batman, villains who were too dangerous and sometimes too insane to be held in regular prisons.

It was Halloween night, and the stillness surrounding Arkham was abruptly disrupted by a loud crash.

*BLAM!*

It was the sound of a giant fist crashing through a wall of the asylum building! Bricks fell to the ground as

Solomon Grundy used the sheer force of his body to smash the rest of the way through, creating a huge, jagged hole in the side of the building.

Standing seven feet tall and weighing 517 pounds, the zombielike Grundy had been one of Batman's strongest and most dangerous enemies, and now the asylum's exterior wall was the only thing that separated him from the innocent people celebrating Halloween in nearby Gotham City. And he wasn't alone.

"Come on!" he yelled behind him as he ran toward the concrete wall that stood between him and the outside world.

"Hold up, Grundy," called a female voice. "I'm coming."

The sorceress Silver Banshee stepped through the hole, her long white hair whipping in the wind and her dead eyes blinking in the moonlight. Silver Banshee possessed superhuman strength and the power to create a sonic boom just by using her voice. As soon as she was free from Arkham, she was going to seek revenge against the heroes who had imprisoned her.

She caught up to Grundy, who was already pounding his massive fist against the concrete wall. He quickly knocked a gaping hole in it, and the two villains stepped through. Solomon Grundy and Silver Banshee quickly disappeared into the woods before anyone even knew they had escaped.

# CHAPTER 2

Meanwhile, in downtown Gotham City the Halloween festivities were in full swing. Giant video screens on the sides of the office buildings were broadcasting images of ghosts and witches. Brightly lit jack-o'-lanterns were displayed in shop windows, and the sidewalks were full of people wearing costumes and carrying trick-or-treat bags. One man, who was dressed as Elvis Presley in sunglasses and a white jumpsuit, bumped into the towering Solomon Grundy. At first the man looked frightened, but then he smiled, assuming Grundy was wearing a remarkably realistic costume.

"Zombie wrestler! Nice one!" the Elvis guessed. Then he high-fived Grundy's giant hand.

As the man walked away, Grundy smiled and turned to Silver Banshee. "Grundy love Halloween!" he said.

*BEEP! BEEP!*

A red convertible had stopped in front of Grundy and Silver Banshee, who were standing in the middle of the street, and the driver was honking the car's horn. The driver was wearing a Batman costume, and the other two passengers were dressed as Green Arrow and Robin.

"Keep it moving, freak show!" yelled the driver.

Silver Banshee glared at the car and said, "Freak show, is it?"

The driver stood up in the car and yelled, "I *said* get out of the street!"

"Well, I hate your hero costumes, and so does my friend," said Silver Banshee.

"Lady, I don't care what you or your—" the driver started to say.

Just then Grundy reached over and easily lifted the car with one hand.

"Ah!" cried the three costumed men as Grundy shook the car and dumped the trio onto the street.

Moments later Silver Banshee was at the wheel of

the convertible, cackling with glee as she and Grundy drove off.

"Faster! Go faster!" yelled Grundy with a big smile on his face.

"Coming up," said Silver Banshee, and she stepped on the gas pedal. They were soon speeding through the streets of Gotham City, weaving recklessly around other cars.

Just then a pair of flying police cars whipped around the corner, in hot pursuit of the stolen convertible. Sirens filled the air as the police vehicles flew closer.

"Policemen!" said Grundy.

"I got this," said Silver Banshee as she turned around to glare at the police cars. "Take the wheel, Grundy."

As Grundy grabbed the steering wheel, Silver Banshee hopped into the backseat of the car. The she opened her mouth and yelled.

The explosive sonic boom of her scream slammed into one of the police cars and sent it spinning through the air and crashing to the ground.

Silver Banshee was panting heavily, trying to catch her breath.

"Why you stop?" asked Grundy.

"I have to catch my breath at some point!" Silver Banshee said angrily.

"Pull over!" came the voice of a policeman over a loudspeaker. "Pull over and give yourself up!"

"Not likely!" said Silver Banshee. Then she drew in her breath and screamed again.

Her voice hit the other police car like a sledgehammer and sent it careening through the air until it smashed into a building.

"Yessss!" yelled Grundy as he raised both of his arms in victory.

"Keep your hands on the wheel, Grundy!" said Silver Banshee.

As the villains sped through downtown Gotham City, a tall figure emerged from the shadows atop a nearby building and watched their progress. It was Nightwing, the skilled crime fighter and one of Batman's closest allies. Nightwing was Dick Grayson and had once been Batman's young partner, Robin. Now Nightwing patrolled Gotham City every night. He tapped a button on the side of his mask, which allowed the cameras within his eyepieces to zoom in on Grundy and Silver Banshee.

Nightwing didn't even turn around when he heard the soft thud of someone landing on the rooftop behind him.

"I'm glad you're here," Nightwing said, thinking Batman had arrived.

"People usually are," said a voice in response.

Nightwing spun around and saw his friend Green Arrow step into the light. Green Arrow was a super hero and an expert archer. Like Nightwing, he often fought crime alongside Batman. Green Arrow was the secret identity of the multimillionaire Oliver Queen.

Nightwing was surprised to see him. "Green Arrow? What are you doing here?"

"Nice to see you again too, kid," Green Arrow said with a grin. "The police subnet said there was an escape at Arkham, and I was in the neighborhood anyway."

"Really?" Nightwing asked skeptically.

"Not even close," admitted Green Arrow as he loaded an arrow into his bow. "But I didn't want to miss the fun."

He shot the arrow into the street below them. It sailed through the air and hit the trunk of the stolen convertible as the car passed by.

"Wait for it," said Green Arrow. "Three, two . . ."

*BLAM!*

The arrow made the trunk of the car explode and sent the convertible spinning out of control. Grundy frantically grasped the steering wheel as Silver Banshee turned to glare at the heroes. She took a deep breath, opened her mouth, and screamed.

"Jump!" yelled Nightwing as her sonic blast slammed into the building below them.

Both men somersaulted through the air and landed on a nearby rooftop, just as Silver Banshee screamed again, this time knocking the heroes off their feet.

"I think I got 'em that time," she said to Grundy.

"Bigger problem," said Grundy. "Object in mirror may be closer than it appears."

Silver Banshee turned around and saw the Batmobile, Batman's turbocharged crime-fighting vehicle, approaching fast. She inhaled deeply, trying to catch her breath.

Batman was driving, and Red Robin was in the passenger seat, pushing buttons on the computer in the vehicle's dashboard. Red Robin was a teen crime fighter, also known as Tim Drake. He was Batman's newest and youngest partner.

"Positive ID," said Red Robin. "It's Solomon Grundy and Silver Banshee."

"Let's see if they want a trick or a treat," said Batman as he accelerated and slammed the Batmobile against the back of the convertible. Silver Banshee was knocked to the floor of the car before she could scream again.

*WHOMP!*

Nightwing fired a grappling line that landed on top of the villains' car. He jumped over Grundy and collided with

Silver Banshee in the backseat. He quickly reached for his two batons, and the tips of his weapons crackled with electricity. Silver Banshee grabbed Nightwing's wrists, so that he had to strain to move the batons toward her.

"Almost there!" called out Grundy from the front seat as they approached a tunnel.

"Step on it, will you?" grunted Silver Banshee as she slammed her knees into Nightwing's stomach and knocked him off balance.

Suddenly a bright green motorcycle zoomed onto the street and pulled up alongside the convertible. It was Green Arrow.

"Trick or treat, snowflake," he called out to Grundy.

Grundy ignored him and sped into the tunnel. As soon as the convertible and Green Arrow were inside, Silver Banshee opened her mouth and screamed.

Huge chunks of the tunnel's cement walls tumbled down and blocked the tunnel entrance completely. As the villains sped deeper into the tunnel, the Batmobile screeched to a halt outside, unable to enter the tunnel because of the rubble.

"Now what?" asked Red Robin.

"Time to do some drilling," said Batman as he pushed a button on the dashboard.

A panel opened at the front of the Batmobile, and a giant, spinning drill bit emerged and started carving through the debris.

Inside the tunnel the villains' car came to a stop as Green Arrow and Nightwing were hit by a sticky green glob that released a toxic gas. Green Arrow coughed and fell off his motorcycle, clasping his head in pain.

Nightwing couldn't move and watched helplessly as Silver Banshee delivered a punch, knocking him unconscious.

A man stepped out of the shadows at the side of the tunnel and stood over Green Arrow. It was the Scarecrow, the deadly villain who had once been a brilliant scientist named Dr. Jonathan Crane. During one of his experiments Crane had developed a fear-inducing gas that caused nightmares in the mind of anyone who inhaled it.

Green Arrow slowly opened his eyes. After one glance at the Scarecrow, he quickly closed them again and started screaming in fear, "No! Get away from me! Get away!"

"Boo!" the Scarecrow said. Then he walked over to Grundy and Silver Banshee and glared at them. "What were you two *doing*?" he asked angrily.

"Don't be mad, Scarecrow," said Grundy with an embarrassed look.

"It was just a joyride," explained Silver Banshee.

"Was the plan too complicated for your pea-brains?" demanded the Scarecrow.

"Brain not made of peas," grumbled Grundy.

"You recall I told you to head directly to the meeting place after your escape? No antics? No tomfoolery? No shenanigans?"

"We remember," said Silver Banshee, sulking.

"*This*, my associates, is the very *definition* of shenanigans!" yelled the Scarecrow as he opened the car door and pushed Grundy aside. "Slide over. I'll drive."

The convertible zoomed out of the tunnel, leaving the two heroes sprawled on the ground.

It wasn't long before the Batmobile bored a hole through the rubble and Batman and Red Robin were able to drive into the tunnel and find their fallen friends.

"Arrow? Can you hear me?" asked Batman, gently tapping Green Arrow's face to wake him up.

Green Arrow moaned in pain and then focused on Batman's face.

"Oh, it's you," he said woozily. "Hey, Bats. I thought you might need some help."

Red Robin checked on Nightwing, who felt like he was waking up from a nightmare. Nightwing tossed what was

left of the green goo over to Batman to analyze.

Batman ran a diagnostic scan on the green glob. "There are endoscopic traces of tetracycline and aerosol still in the air," he said. "That's residue from the Scarecrow's fear gas."

"Scarecrow, Silver Banshee, and Grundy are all working together?" asked Red Robin.

Batman looked grim. "Happy Halloween," he said.

Looking for another great book?
Find it
**IN THE MIDDLE**.

Fun, fantastic books for kids
in the in-be**TWEEN** age.

IntheMiddleBooks.com

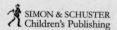